ALUKA
The Seventh Day Ser
By Leslie Sv

Copyright 2020, Leslie Swartz

Library of Congress Control Number: 2020912588

ISBN: 9798663979627

Too long a sacrifice can make a stone of a heart.

William Butler Yeats

Prologue

The man spilled thirty silver coins onto the sorcerer's table and tucked his long hair behind his ears. "Give me something to ease my guilt, shopkeeper. And, if no such thing exists, give me something to end my suffering for I am shamed and pained by wretched remorse."

The sorcerer could see the anguish in the man's eyes and took pity on him. "I have something," he said, reaching into a basket under the table. "It will not take away what you are feeling, but it will give you time to make amends. Is that what you want? To make things right?"

"I see no way of righting what I have done. My sin is far too great. But, if there *is* a way, I will have what you are selling."

"Very well." He held out an ornate bottle no larger than his index finger kept closed with a tiny piece of cork.

"A potion?" the man asked, taking the bottle and opening it, smelling the contents, and giving the sorcerer a suspicious glance. "Is this sheep's blood?"

"I assure you, it is not. Drink it and you will have your redemption."

Desperate, the man emptied the bottle into his throat, swallowing fast, hoping to avoid the salty iron taste of the deep red fluid. He placed the bottle on the table and cringed. He nodded to the sorcerer, left the bottle and the silver, and exited the shop, feeling no better than when he'd entered.

He sat under the tree, its deep pink flowers seeming to mock him with their beauty, demanding he be happy when he could not be. He wailed, letting the tears stream down his face uninterrupted as he sobbed. He labored to breathe as his stomach ached, his guilt and grief overwhelming. "Tell me what to do," he prayed, looking to the sky. "I will do anything you command. Give me a task and I shall complete it. What must I do to appease you?"

The clouds parted, opening up to the clear and starry night. The moon revealed itself and in its light, he could see a discarded rope lying on the ground a few feet away. He stood, walked over, and picked it up. "Is this what you demand of me, Lord?" His voice quivered as he worked the rope into a noose. "Shall this be my punishment?" He threw it over the sturdiest branch and tied it in place. "I can not be certain if you wish it, but I would rather feel the agony of death than live with the grievous sin I have committed. Please forgive me, Lord, and if you can not, know that I understand, for in this life and the next, I will never forgive myself." He climbed up the tree, sending the sparrows fleeing from their nests, placed the rope around his neck, and let go.

A group of men with torches came storming through the forest, calling for the man to show himself. Hungry for justice, they were stopped in their tracks when they saw the body hanging, limp, its eyes bulged and its tongue protruding.

"It's The Betrayer!" one of the men yelled upon closer inspection.

"Are you sure?" another asked.

"Yes! I'd recognize him anywhere, even in this state. The coward took his own life."

"How will we have justice *now*?"

"We will cut him down and bury his body in Akeldama."

"But, that's for foreigners."

"He was a stranger to us, was he not? Did we know what he was capable of? Did he share his plans with any of us? No. He did what he did in secret. He hid who he truly was from all of us. Akeldama is what he deserves."

3

The men took the body to the field, dug a hole, and dropped it in. They covered it and left it unmarked, spitting on it before turning to leave.

"Mmmff."

"Did you hear that?" one of the men asked.

"Hear what?" another responded.

"Mmmff."

"That."

"I did."

"As did I," another chimed in. The men turned, realizing that the sound was coming from the grave. They stared, horror covering their faces as their hearts began to race.

"Was he still alive?" the first man wondered.

"He couldn't have been," the second said. "Could he?"

The earth seemed to breathe, pulsating under the light of the full moon. The men watched in terror as one hand, then two appeared from underneath the soil.

"We buried him alive," one man uttered.

He clawed his way out, the others too stunned to move. He rose, the dirt falling away from his clothes as he climbed out and stood upright. "What has happened?"

The men stayed silent.

"What have you done to me?"

"You were dead," one of them told him. "We thought."

His mind went dark, his thoughts replaced by instinct alone. The sound of pounding in his ears was so incessant, he could hear nothing else. His eyes went black and his teeth seemed to grow, causing the others to scream and run. He chased them down, one by one, ripping out their throats with his newly formed fangs. The taste on his lips whipped him into a frenzy. He needed more of the salty liquid covering his mouth. His eyes shined in the moonlight as he bent over the dying men, clamped down on one neck after another, and drank. When the last man was dead, the pounding stopped. As he came to his senses, he realized that the noise he'd been hearing must have been their heartbeats. He stood in horror, looking down at the men he used to call friends. "What have I done?" he whispered, wiping the blood from his face. "What am I?"

He burst into the shop, filthy and covered in other men's blood. "Charlatan!" he shouted, startling the shopkeeper. "You offer no redemption. You've made me a demon!"

"Not a demon," the sorcerer corrected. "You are now as I am. Alukah."

His face went hot as he bounded toward the table. "You've made me a monster! An abomination!"

"I only gave you the option. Had you remained alive, no change would have befallen you."

"Take it away! Return me to my true self."

"This is who you are. There is no going back. Don't you understand? I've given you what you wanted."

"I did *not* ask for this."

"*Time*. So long as you stay out of the sun and keep your head and your heart, you will live forever. No matter how long it takes, you will one day find the redemption you seek. In the meantime, you'll possess strength beyond measure. Women will fall at your feet. Those things may seem fleeting, but they will be a source of happiness for you until you get the--"

The man gripped the sorcerer's throat, his rage once again taking over. He pulled out his trachea, the sound of his voice having become too irritating to take. He broke a chair over the shopkeeper's head, shattering it to pieces. He picked up one of the chair legs, leaped on top of him, and plunged it into the sorcerer's heart. When he'd gone still, the man got up and began to run.

He ran all night, faster than he'd ever run before. Faster than anyone should have been able to. He ran until he found himself in a country he didn't recognize in a tiny village on the other side of the Salt Sea. He felt weak, tired, and hungry. He sought refuge in an inn, but the keeper refused him, not recognizing his speech. Exhausted and overcome with what felt like starvation, he pounced, drinking the innkeeper dry before moving on, going from one room to the next, killing everyone in the building. Yet unsatisfied, he blew through the village, killing man, woman, and child, from house to house, feasting on an abundance of blood and misery. When he was finished, there was no one left. The village was dead.

He returned to the inn, the threat of sunrise upon him. He hid in the kitchen, the only room with no windows, found a bag of grain to put under his head, and went to sleep, his guilt rising in his chest as he drifted off. His slumber was restless, the screams of his victims emblazoned in his subconscious. He had nightmares of their cries, of their faces and he'd continue to have the same horrific dreams every day for the remainder of his life.

Chapter 1

Phindi walked the halls of the converted fortress, the vampires in her keep all quiet in their beds as the sun made its fiery rise above the thick, stone castle. Dated to 1477, she'd chosen the citadel in Alexandria as her command center for its strategic location. Centered between the two realms she now governed, Egypt was the perfect place to bridge her lands and monitor the happenings in both. There were rumors of someone calling himself 'King', but nothing substantiated, so she had her best spies out every night hunting for proof. In the meantime, she did her duty as Duchess by mediating disputes, paying the bills of those in her charge, overseeing the renovation of the building she occupied, and filling it with flame lilies. She couldn't stand most flowers. She found them frivolous and distracting, but she knew to be an effective leader she would have to be more than the Queen's general. She'd have to be seen not only as a warrior but as an ally, someone that cared about her people's problems and someone that they could relate to. Decorating her residence was one way of showing a softer side of herself, even if no such side existed, and flame lilies, while beautiful, are highly poisonous which Phindi saw as their one redeeming quality.

As she headed to her rooms, she heard a crash coming from the main hall followed by what sounded like a hundred men screaming. She looked down over the railing of the loft to the grand room below. The main entrance had been broken through and men poured in by the dozens, all cloaked in forest green and shouting, "For the King!" They wielded sleek, steel spikes, some burning their hands as they unsheathed them, the room now flooded with early morning daylight. They bounded up the stone staircase, determined, like hunters searching out their prey. Phindi took three seconds to get her bearings as she acclimated to her current predicament. Her home, her sanctuary, her fortress was being invaded.

"Rebels!" she boomed through the halls, pounding on the doors of the sleeping loyalists. She rushed to the armory at the end of the hallway, pulling swords and spears from their places on the walls and turning back to distribute them to her people, but by the time she'd returned, the fighting had already begun.

Half of the loyalists were slaughtered in their beds while the rest fought barehanded against the armed force, tearing heads from bodies and throwing their attackers over the railing. Phindi tossed weapons to her subordinates, leaving none for herself. She flew at the rebels, fangs bared, her arms outstretched. She drove her sharp nails into their abdomens, yanking out intestines before reaching up into their chests and clawing out their hearts.

As more men flooded the building, a voice came from behind. "Your Grace!" Phindi turned to see one of her fledglings holding her assegai. "Forgive me. I went into your rooms to retrieve it." The girl held it out to her and she took it, nodding in approval.

Above the entrance hung a massive banner, rolled up and largely ignored. Phindi leaped up onto the railing, took aim, and threw her spear at the gold cord holding it in place. The banner fell, its deep purple velvet blocking out the sun's rays, enabling the loyalists to descend, meeting the intruders in less confining quarters. They pounced, hacking off heads and running rebels through with their swords. Phindi leaped through the air, pulling her spear from the wall and landing confidently on her feet. She took her weapon in both hands, using it as a blunt instrument with which to knock her opponent to the ground before raising it above her head, her foot on the man's throat.

"Who sent you?" she demanded.

The man laughed, blood dribbling from the corner of his mouth. "My King."

"Who? Who is this self-proclaimed King that blasphemes against our Queen?"

"He is our redeemer. He saves us from your bitch Queen's tyranny."

Her eyes widened as her anger grew. "Your disrespect will not go unpunished. Know that on this day, you dishonor not the Queen, but yourself." She brought the spear down hard, sinking it in his chest and through his heart. His eyes went dim, the last bit of life leaving him. She pulled out the assegai and surveyed the room. A handful of her people remained, their shoulders slumped as they grieved the loss of their friends. Everyone else was dead. "Go to your rooms," she commanded. "It is day and you are exhausted."

"Will you inform the Queen of this treachery?" one of the girls asked.

"Yes, but not until I can offer her a solution to the problem. I will find out where this 'King' hides while he sends others to fight his battles. I will gather troops. I will form a plan and with Her Majesty's blessing, I will root out the traitor and scorch the earth to cleanse him from it."

The vampires bowed and scurried back up the steps to their rooms, locking themselves in for the day. Phindi looked over the bodies, spear in hand, resentment building like a wall in her chest, hard and strong. She would raise her army. She would find this King. She would have her revenge.

Chapter 2

"Can I come in?" Gabriel asked, her eyes bloodshot and her expression grim.

Wyatt stepped aside, closing the door behind her as she entered. "You knocked."

"Yeah."

"Have you ever knocked on a door in your life?"

"Once or twice. Can I talk to you?"

"Sure. I was about to have coffee. You want some?"

She cringed. He poured himself a cup, the morning sun lighting up the apartment in a flood of golden radiance.

"You sure? You look exhausted."

"I haven't slept."

"Soda?"

She nodded. He set his cup down and got the caffeinated beverage from the fridge. He slid it across to her as they sat at the island and she opened it, downing half the can before stopping to take a breath.

"So, what's going on? Another crisis? You need me to throw a ball of lightning at a Kraken or something?"

She shook her head, eyes fixed on the soda can.

"Lucifer giving you a hard time?"

She let out a grieved sigh. "No, Lucifer's probably dead."

He choked on his coffee. "Dead? Of what?"

"Oh, you know, not listening. I mean, I'm not *sure*, but I can't feel him anymore, so I'm assuming he's not on Earth, which means he's dead."

"Holy shit."

"That's not what I want to talk to you about, though."

"It's not? Because that's a pretty big deal."

"It's not. Listen, I don't normally talk to you about my problems because I don't want to burden you. You have enough to deal with. But, I can't go to Uriel with this without upsetting Sinclair, Wendy isn't back from New Zealand, and Lucifer's gone, so--"

"Hey," he said, reaching across the island and putting his hand over hers. "You can *always* talk to me."

She nodded, tears forming in her eyes. She looked up at him as they spilled down her cheeks. "I'm afraid you'll hate me."

"I won't," he promised, the pain on her face breaking his heart.

"I hope that's true." She brushed away her tears and took a deep breath before beginning. "When I was fifteen, my parents killed me…twice, after they killed my girlfriend and her family."

"Jesus Christ."

"Yeah. Pushed me down a flight of stairs, broke my neck. Then, shot me in the heart. My best friend saw it happen and he lost control. He killed them. He's been in prison for the last twenty years. He *was* in prison…until last night." She took a sip of soda, preparing herself to continue. "We met when we were ten. My parents took me to the city to see A Christmas Carol on Broadway. He was outside the theater panhandling, homeless, so I convinced James and Ester to bring him home. He stayed with us for a few days until my mom called social services and they took him away. He got put in foster care and I was scared I'd never see him again, so I ran away to find him. He was just a few streets over, so no one even realized I'd gone. We were inseparable for years after that. He took care of me when Ester would hit me or I'd get overwhelmed by all the thoughts in my head that weren't mine. He moved in after the Murphys' funeral so I wouldn't be alone. He waited until I found Uri and Raph. But, then he turned himself in. He was afraid he would hurt me or someone else. He was having a hard time reigning in who he was."

"Who he was?"

She sniffed as she fought to control her emotions. "He was one of us, B. Camael. The Wrath of God."

He raised his eyebrows. "Oh. So, he's out now?"

"He was." She wiped away more tears as she explained. "I visited him every week for the last twenty years. I told him everything that was going on with you and the others. I told him everything about everything. I grew up with him. He knew me, you know? And then, God came calling." Her tone turned resentful as she took another drink and slammed the can back on the counter.

"God? He spoke to you?"

"No, He just downloads information to my brain like a fucking laptop whenever He sees fit. It's pretty unpleasant. When I found out where Dia's descendants were, I also found out what Cam's purpose here was." She covered her mouth as she held back sobs. Unable to stifle her emotions, she continued through the tears, her voice going up an octave as she moved from the island to the sofa, sitting down and hugging her arms as if she were cold. "I had to tell him to break out of prison, drag him to a fight, and watch him die doing God's work. I had to burn his body so he could go home. I killed him, B. I killed my best friend."

He sat next to her on the couch and wrapped his arms around her shoulders, kissing the top of her head. "You didn't kill him."

"I did. *I did.* Because God commanded it. I always do what He wants me to. I *always* make it happen. Whatever it is that He wants done, I get that shit done. And I understand. The greater good and all that, but *fuck.*" She put her hand to her diaphragm as it got harder for her to breathe.

He held her closer, rubbing her arm, tears in his eyes now, as well. She made so much more sense to him now as a person. The weight of what God put on her, the responsibility, and the sacrifice. The abusive parents and traumatic childhood. He was amazed she hadn't fallen apart before now.

She cried into his chest for a few minutes, eventually calming down enough to have the hard part of the conversation. "There's more." She sat back, looking him in the eye, watching his expressions carefully, afraid of how he'd react. "The thing God wanted Cam to do," She paused, taking a shaky breath. "Was to kill Cain."

Wyatt's eyes grew wide, moving from his sister to the bedroom door where Allydia slept. "Cain killed him?"

"No, not exactly. Anything physically harmful that happens to Cain happens to whoever inflicted the damage times seven. God's Wrath is the only thing strong enough to kill him permanently, so when Cam killed Cain, he died, too."

"Oh, shit." He rubbed his chin. "I don't know how she's gonna feel about that."

"Relieved, I imagine. He was a shit father *before* he kidnapped her kids, called her a monster, and threatened to murder her. He's the reason she got all paranoid and hired a bunch of spies. She was scared he was coming after her."

"Then, why did you think I'd hate you? If you were doing what God forced you to and Allydia won't be hurt, why would I be angry?"

"Not about Cain. About the party."

He tilted his head. "What party?"

"In '97. Crystal something-or-other's birthday. East 48th street."

"Crystal Bowers. I remember that. Well, bits and pieces. I got pretty wasted that night."

"I'm so sorry." She sniffed again as more tears threatened to come.

"For what?"

"I was there. I saw you with that girl, standing by the speaker, beer in your hand. I watched you take her into a room and close the door. I knew who you were and I didn't say anything."

He went quiet, his expression somber, his eyes fixed on hers.

"I had a problem back then. I couldn't always handle the voices. Everyone's thoughts and feelings. It was a lot. And after my parents killed Ada, my girlfriend, my issue got out of control. I was, um," She wanted to look away, but she couldn't. She needed to see his reaction. "I was on heroin."

His features softened and he looked down at his hands in his lap.

"That night, I shot up more than a normal person would've been able to take. I was limp on the couch. I could barely make words. I couldn't hear your thoughts or feel your feelings, but I knew you were my brother. I didn't know your human name, but I was sure that you were Barachiel, Protector of Humanity, Leader of the Guardians, Angel of

Blessings. *I knew it* and I just lay there, wallowing in my own bullshit. I'm so sorry, B. If I had known what would happen--"

"But, you didn't, did you?" He looked her in the eyes again. "You couldn't have. Not unless He wanted you to."

"I was stoned. I shouldn't have been. I should have been more responsible. I should have taken it more seriously."

"Taken what more seriously?"

"Who I am."

They were quiet for a moment while Wyatt gathered his thoughts. She'd expected him to be angry, but he wasn't. All she could feel him feeling for her was love and pity.

"I'm not mad at you, Gabriel. You were a kid with maybe the worst parents of all time plus *everyone* in your head. I can't imagine what that must be like."

She brushed away a final tear. "You don't hate me."

"No," he smiled. "Did I ever tell you how I met my wife?"

She knew the story, given that she knew everything about him as soon as she set eyes on him at his therapist's office a few years before, but she shook her head, knowing that he wanted to tell it.

"On nine-eleven, I was at my college's counselor's office not because I was upset about what had happened, but because I was seeing the ghosts of people that were killed. I thought I was having a meltdown. It was the worst 'hallucination' I'd ever had. So I was sitting there, waiting my turn, people crying all around me, and in walks Annie, calm as can be, carrying a twenty-four pack of water in her hands and a tote bag full of brownies she'd made over her shoulder. She gave everyone in the office a brownie and a bottle and asked if they were okay. She hugged people she'd never met and talked to them until they relaxed. She got to me last, gave me two brownies. Said I looked like I needed them more than anyone else there. She sat with me for *two hours* talking about everything and nothing. She made me laugh. She made me forget for a while that I was crazy. By the time it was my turn to see the counselor, the ghosts were gone and I felt fine. I think I fell in love with her right there." He tilted his head to make sure she was paying attention before he continued. "If you had told me who I was, *what* I was, I would have avoided two decades of mental illness and everything that went with it. But, I also would never have been in that counselor's office. I wouldn't have met Annie. I wouldn't have had Will."

She bit her bottom lip. "Do you think it would have been better that way? I know how much losing them hurt you."

"No," he insisted. "I would rather feel the pain of losing them every day than go through my entire life never having loved them. So, I don't blame you for ignoring me at that party. Whether it was God's will or just dumb luck, it doesn't matter. I'm grateful to have had them. No matter what happened, I know that they loved me."

She looked toward the bedroom door and back at him. "You know, Dia loves you, too. Hard."

"Does she?"

"*Hard*. Girl is all in. I haven't seen her like this ever. And, me and Uriel love you. And Sinclair. Not in the same gag-inducing way the vampire Queen does, but we do."

He laughed.

"So, don't go thinking there aren't people that care about you. And I don't give a fuck what happens from now until my feathery ass is back in Heaven, don't you even think about committing suicide again. My heart can't take it."

"I won't, I swear," he chuckled.

"Good. Is it okay if I take a nap on your couch? I'm stupid tired."

"Go ahead. I'll get you a pillow." He went to the hall closet, taking out a spare pillow and throw blanket. He set the pillow on one end of the couch and she immediately dropped her head onto it, curling up in the fetal position as he covered her with the blanket.

"Thanks, B. Love you."

"Love you, too." He went back to the island and finished his coffee, watching his sister sleep, having a new appreciation for her now that he knew what she'd been through. He'd always thought Annie was the strongest person he'd ever known, but he was wrong. Gabriel was.

Chapter 3

"Daddy," the small voice said, waking Malik from a dead sleep. "Daddy, wake up." He looked to his right and saw Valerie lying there, eyes closed, still asleep. "Daddy!" He jumped, finally seeing the girl at the side of the bed. She looked to be three or four years old, long, curly hair flowing down her back, wearing one of his wife's tee-shirts as a nightgown.

"What the..." He sat up, rubbing his eyes and turning on the light.

"Daddy, can you make eggs for breakfast?" the girl asked sweetly.

He stared, mouth agape. It took him several seconds to come to terms with who she was as it was just the night before that she'd taken her first steps. "Sinclair?"

She nodded. "Scrambled. And strawberries? Strawberries are my favorite."

"Um, sure, baby. Just let me get woken up. I'll be right there."

"Okay. Hurry, though." Her pupils dilated completely causing Malik's heart to jump to his throat. "I'm hungry." She skipped out of the room leaving him in a cold sweat. He looked back at a still sleeping Valerie, his heart thumping. She was oblivious and he was petrified.

"Mommy!" Sinclair cheered as Valerie entered the living room, Malik following closely behind.

"Holy shit," the mother muttered under her breath. The girl ran to her, putting her arms up to be held. Valerie complied, picking her up and carrying her on her hip to the dining table. "Looks like I'm gonna have to go shopping. You've outgrown all your clothes!"

Sinclair laughed.

"You'll need a big girl bed, too. Daddy said you want eggs for breakfast?"

"Yeah! And strawberries. And orange juice. And toast!"

"Oh! Okay, well, you heard her," she said to Malik who had already begun work in the kitchen. She turned her attention back to her daughter as she got her sat in a chair. "We'll have to get shoes and barrettes and headbands. Maybe after breakfast, we can braid your hair, how's that sound?"

"Yay!" the child beamed, clapping her hands and bouncing in her seat. "Can we also get some crayons? I really wanna draw."

"Of course! Crayons, finger paint, construction paper, all that stuff."

"Thank you, Mommy!"

Malik set plates in front of them and went back to the kitchen for the juice. As he poured, he glanced over at the table, watching anxiously as they ate. Maybe he'd been seeing things. It was early and he'd just woken up. But he knew what he saw. Her eyes had gone black. He was *sure*. According to his wife, that's something vampires did when they were about to bite someone. Had Sinclair been threatening him? Or was she just too young to control her instincts? Either way, between that and the hyper-fast aging, he was freaked out. *Get it together*, he thought, placing the cups in front of his wife and daughter. *This is your new normal. Learn to live with it.*

Chapter 4

"Well, that's good," Gabriel muttered as she peeked her head into Lucifer's room and found it empty. The sheets were stained with blood, but the bed was unoccupied, which meant that he'd recovered from the injuries he'd received during his bout with Cain. She shuffled to the kitchen, hoping there were some cookies left in the pantry, but as she passed the living room, she caught a glimpse of Lucifer on her balcony and he wasn't alone.

"What in the actual fuck?" she snapped as she went to meet him. On the floor between them lay what looked like a half-reanimated corpse, bloated, worms crawling out of its nose, moaning in anguish.

"Surprise!" Lucifer gleaned, clearly proud of himself. "It's our nephew. Well, it will be, once you heal his body. In retrospect, it may have been kinder to acquire him a fresh one, but in my excitement, I shoved his soul right back into the original. Must be unbearably painful."

"Jesus, Lucifer." She covered her mouth at the stench coming from the body. "He would have been reincarnated." She held her hand out, using her telekinesis to pull embalming fluid, muddy water, worms, and insects from the boy's stomach and lungs. He groaned, convulsing as the thread that had been keeping his eyes sewn shut broke, his milky eyes bulging.

"Yes, eventually, long after you all died and had gone back home. Losing Mariana has given me a new appreciation for human grief. Barachiel needs his son back *now*. Besides, don't you find it odd that the boy existed at all?"

"This is taking forever," she huffed as more and more sludge came seeping out of Will's nose and mouth.

"Don't you see? After my skirmish with Cain, I should have gone back to Hell, but I landed in Purgatory. *Purgatory*. I have no human soul. There was no reason for me to have ended up there. There's no explanation other than God made it so. He *must* want Will alive. Think about it, sister. There's no way our brother should have been able to procreate unless our Father wanted him to."

She sighed as the last of the fluid drained from Will's body. She placed her hands on his head and heart, his skin glowing from the inside at the touch. After a few moments, his appearance changed from a swollen, green, and gray zombie to the young man Gabriel had seen in Wyatt's memories. His eyes cleared, returning to their natural, grayish hue and color returned to his cheeks. He grasped her wrist, looking up at her in terror.

"You're all right," she assured him, helping him to sit up.

As he acclimated to his senses, he opened his mouth to speak. At first, only scratchy, broken syllables escaped his throat, but after a few seconds, words finally came. "Au-- Aunt Gabriel?"

She nodded, tears forming in her eyes.

"What-- How?"

"My doing," Lucifer chirped.

He turned his head to see his uncle standing behind him. On instinct, he heaved a bolt of lightning in his direction. Lucifer stepped aside to avoid getting hit.

"Feisty as ever, I see."

"Yo," Gabriel lectured, taking Will's hand and resting it by his side. "None of that."

He shifted his gaze back to her. "I was dead, wasn't I?"

"Yes," Lucifer told him. "It was unsightly. Very grim. I really should have taken a photograph."

Gabriel shot him a look before answering. "You were, but Lucifer brought you back."

"Is he stupid?"

"Kind of." She helped him up, his legs wobbling like a newborn deer as he stood.

"I resent that," Lucifer piped. "Just because you don't know why he was born, doesn't mean there isn't a reason."

"You have no idea what I know."

"I shouldn't be here," Will said, eyeing the railing. "After what I did, I don't deserve to--"

"What is with you people wanting to die?" Gabriel asked. "Seriously, is it something in your genes? Honestly. I have been through a lot of shit and I have never once wanted to fling myself from a building. *I'm a trash can* and I still love myself."

"Not the worst way to go," Lucifer interjected. "Certainly less painful than slicing open your wrists with a piece of broken glass. Then again, your father always has been a bit of a drama queen."

Will formed a ball of electricity in his hand as he stared his uncle down. "My father was a fucking saint. If I hear you disrespecting him again, I swear to God."

"He's alive," Gabriel told him.

The energy in his hand dissipated as his features softened. "What?"

"Yeah, Dia drinking so much of his blood when they first hooked up made him basically immortal. It's a whole thing."

"Is he," he stopped, choking back tears. "Is he okay?"

"Eh, better than he was."

"Where is he?"

"At his dad's place."

"I want to see him. I have to tell him I'm sorry. I have to--" He stumbled as he tried to take a step. Gabriel caught him and helped him walk inside.

"All right, kid. I'll take you to him. Shower first, though. You're covered in all manner of crap and you smell like a dumpster."

He nodded.

"You can borrow some of your uncle's clothes until we get you some new ones, *can't he?*"

"Of course," Lucifer agreed. "What's mine is yours. As long as I can be there when we surprise Barachiel."

"Yes, fine." She opened the door to the hall bathroom and took Will's face in her hands. "You know I love you, right?"

"Yeah. I love you, too."

"Good. So don't make me regret not letting you yeet yourself into traffic, okay?"

He nodded.

She brushed away a tear and hugged him. "I missed you."

He went into the bathroom and closed the door. When she heard the water running, Gabriel went back to join her brother in the living room. "You are dumb as shit."

"What?" he chuckled.

She pointed out onto the mess on the floor of the balcony. "You're cleaning that up."

Chapter 5

As night fell, Allydia emerged from Wyatt's bedroom already stunning in her leather pants and deep v-neck, cold-shoulder top. He wanted to scoop her up and take her right back to bed, but he couldn't let himself get distracted. He had to tell her about her father and he wasn't sure how she was going to take the news.

"Hey," he greeted as she sat next to him on the sofa. "You sleep okay?"

"As well as could be expected, I suppose."

"How are you feeling about Navid and everything?"

"All right. He's safe and that's what matters."

He rested his arm behind her on the back of the couch. "Gabriel was here today."

"I know. I can smell her on your furniture. Like chamomile and candy bars."

He fought the urge to laugh. "Something happened. Your father--"

"Are you hurt?" she fussed, looking him over.

"No, I wasn't there. But, baby, God's Wrath was."

"Wrath? You mean fire and brimstone, Sodom and Gomorrah, The Wrath of God? The angel Camael?"

"Yes."

She sat back and folded her arms. "I only met him once, in Hobah. Anger issues."

He placed a hand on her leg as he tried to find the words.

She tucked her hair behind her ears and held his hand. "Cain is dead, isn't he?"

"Yeah, baby, he is. I'm sorry."

She shook her head and put her fingers to his lips, a broken smile appearing on her otherwise solemn face. "I'm fine."

He kissed her hand. "Are you sure? I know what it's like to lose--"

"Our fathers were not the same. It's sweet of you to worry, but you don't have to. I spent centuries looking over my shoulder, afraid and hiding from him. The knowledge of his passing makes me feel," she thought for a moment. "Well, similar to how I feel when I'm with you."

He raised his eyebrows. "How's that?"

She touched his cheek and kissed him softly. "Safe." Her phone buzzed in her back pocket. She took it out to see a text from Hartley. "I have to go." She kissed him again and headed for the door. "I'll be back before you go to bed."

"See you then," he said as she closed the door behind her.

Yo, B, he heard in his head.

Gabriel, he replied. *You okay?*

Relatively. Is your girl with you?

She just left, why?

We're coming over.

Who's we?

You'll see.

"We're getting reports of rebel attacks all over Europe," Hartley said as she bowed her head and followed Allydia up to the throne room, walking through the path cleared by the crowd of vampires that danced on the main floor of the club. "Fires in the hotels in Barcelona and Prague. The nightclubs in Hamburg and Zurich. The brothel in Amsterdam is *gone*. Governors are reporting mass casualties. Numbers are still coming in, but--"

"How can this be?" she barked as they entered the room. Hartley closed the door and knelt before her. "There are plans for things like this. Contingencies. Every Governor is well-armed with stockpiles of weapons to distribute to their people. Every one of my children is well trained in self-defense. How are the rebels doing this?"

"They're attacking in the day, Your Majesty."

"They're *what*?"

"The day. They're cloaking themselves, risking death to butcher us in our sleep. No one is safe, my Queen. Not even under the sun."

"They're mad."

"They're organized. Someone is leading them. There are rumors of someone calling himself 'King'. I have people looking into it, but it seems that this person is ordering simultaneous attacks that are being carried out by those loyal to him. There are more traitors than we thought, Your Majesty. A lot more."

She paced the floor, arms crossed, her brow furrowed in thought and rage. "Call the Governors. All of them. Bring them here for an emergency conference. Offer assistance to whoever needs it and *find me this 'King'*."

"Yes, Your Majesty. I do have one piece of good news. We found the girl, Hattie's Sired. We have her downstairs."

"Show me."

They went back down the staircase to the main floor and opened the door to the lower level. They followed the steps down to a dimly lit room with damp, stone floors and cage-lined walls housing an army's-worth of various weapons. On the far side of the room sat a refrigerator with a stockpile of blood bags and opposite that was a cell. She could see the girl inside, huddled in a corner, and trembling.

Hartley handed Allydia a phone that was not her own, but that of the Queen's former assistant. "This is how we found her. My guys took this off Hattie in Scotland. The girl's was the only number that was ever called. Wasn't hard to trace."

"Thank you, Hartley. That will be all."

"Yes, Your Majesty." She bowed and hurried off to begin making calls.

"Your name is Michelle, yes?" she asked as she walked to the fridge, took a blood bag from it, and tossed it into the cell. The girl scrambled to get it open as fast as she could and guzzled the contents. Allydia tossed her another.

"Yes," the girl confirmed. "Michelle Iha."

"Do you know who I am?"

She nodded as she downed the contents of the second bag.

"I had your maker killed. It pained me, but it was necessary to maintain order. There's a faction of our kind that would see me removed. I can't allow any sign of weakness, do you understand?"

Again, she nodded, clearly frightened.

"There's an uprising I have to attend to, so for now, you'll remain here. When things have settled, I'll consider what to do with you more permanently." She spun on her heel and left the girl alone in the dungeon. Michelle leaned against the wall, crying into its cool stone. Hattie was gone and she was alone.

Chapter 6

Wyatt exited the bathroom to find Gabriel and Lucifer standing in his living room. "Oh, good," he said. "You're alive."

"I'm not the only one," Lucifer smirked, gesturing toward the kitchen. There, eating a piece of leftover pizza straight from the fridge, was Will. He turned to look at his father, dropped his food, and rushed toward him, throwing his arms around him in a tight embrace.

"I'm so sorry, Dad," the boy cried. "I'm so, so sorry."

Wyatt's eyes met Gabriel's, hope and confusion filling them as he all but begged her in his mind for this to be true. She nodded, giving him a reassuring smile. Tears streamed down his face as he hugged him, cradling the back of his head as he kissed his temple. He took his son's face in his hands and looked him over, shock giving way to curiosity. "How?"

"You're welcome," Lucifer chimed.

"You did this?"

"Of course. What are brothers for if not taking an excursion to the afterlife to rescue one's offspring from centuries of solitary torture? Now, if you'll excuse me, I haven't eaten since yesterday and I'm positively famished. Sister, will you be joining me?"

"Yeah, let's give these two some time to catch up." She waved her hand to get Wyatt's attention. *I know you want to tell him about Sinclair, but Michelle should. I'll call her.*

Okay, he agreed.

The two left, leaving father and son alone to talk. Wyatt still couldn't believe it. He didn't want to take his eyes off of Will for a second for fear that he would disappear. "Are you okay?" he asked, his voice shaking. "How do you feel?"

"Guilty," Will told him, tears spilling down his cheeks. "Sad. Disgusted with myself. I am so sorry, Dad. I don't know how to even *start* making things right. Is there a way? Because I'll do anything. Tell me how to fix it and I *will* because I don't--" he paused, stifling a sob. "I don't want you to hate me."

"Hey, I could never hate you, do you hear me?" He held his son's gaze, making sure he understood. "Grandpa was an accident. I know that. And, I can't die, so kill me again, kill me ten more times. I'll always come back and I'll always forgive you. *I'm* sorry. What Barachiel did to you," He sniffed and wiped away a tear. "I'm sorry."

"He was right, though. I'm a hazard. I threatened Lucifer with lightning twice in the first ten minutes I was back and he was the one that saved me."

"To be fair, I threaten Lucifer with lightning on a pretty regular basis. I wouldn't worry too much about it. He usually deserves it."

They both laughed.

"But, Michelle didn't," Will said, his features falling in despair. "I got mad that she told Gabriel I was losing it. I was upset that she was sent there to spy on me and I--" He covered his mouth as fresh tears poured down his cheeks. He took his hand away, trying to control his breathing as he spoke. "I just wanted her to leave me alone. I didn't mean to."

"Hey, hey, it's okay. Michelle's okay."

"What?" he whimpered. "I didn't kill her? I checked. She didn't have a pulse."

"Well, she did die, but she came right back...as a vampire."

Will's eyes were like saucers as he sat on a barstool at the island. "How is she?"

"I don't know. All right, I think."

"I need to see her. Where is she?"

"Relax, Gabriel's calling her now."

She set the phone back on the table as the waiter placed a plate in front of her. "Thank you," she said as he walked off. She took a bite of lasagna and tapped her fork against the plate, her eyes glued to the dark screen on her cellphone.

"What's got you in a mood now, Gabriel?" Lucifer asked, taking a sip of water.

"She's not answering."

"Who isn't?"

"Doesn't matter. Listen, I know I'm kind of dickish, but I'm really glad you're not dead."

"Well, thank you. I'm touched."

"For real, yesterday was a rolling dumpster fire and I'm really happy you survived it."

"What happened?"

"Camael killed Cain, like, for good."

"Wrath was here? I'm sorry I missed him. We had some good times in the old days. So, Camael's back in Heaven, then? I can't imagine him making it out of that alive."

"Yeah, he went back."

"And that displeases you?"

"Obvs."

"You were close?"

"Yeah."

"Well, then, I'm sorry. You will see him again, though. And, silver lining, the pebble in my shoe that was Cain, son of Adam, is finally no more. That's a good thing."

"I guess."

"And that was what I advised you to put off? Telling our fly-off-the-handle brother to do his duty?"

"Yep."

"Is it terrible that I'm glad you didn't listen to me?"

"Maybe a little, but I understand. Cain needed to be put down."

"Like a dog in the street." He raised his glass and took another sip.

"Like you would ever kill a dog."

"No, I wouldn't, but you know who I would kill, over and over again, no matter the consequences had our brother not stepped in?"

She rolled her eyes and sighed. "Cain."

"Cain. Cheers with me, sister." He picked up his glass again. "To Camael, always good for a laugh and the one and only Wrath of the Almighty."

She lifted her glass and clinked it to his, her enthusiasm lacking.

"Come, now. You know he's happy where he is."

"I know. I'm not worried about him, I just miss him." She took another bite as Lucifer cut into his eggplant Parmesan.

"It would seem, then, that we are both grieving the loss of someone we cared for. Perhaps we should form a support group. We could call it, 'Angels with Angst'. I'm sure we could recruit Barachiel to join. He's always distraught over one thing or another."

She snickered and took a sip of soda. "I am sorry about Mariana. She didn't deserve that."

"Yes, well, she too is in a better place. I know because I looked for her while I was in Purgatory and didn't find her."

"That's good, I guess."

"Yes. It's a dreadful place, that. I don't recommend taking an excursion there if you can avoid it."

"I'll keep that in mind."

"I've never felt something so empty. So completely devoid of--"

"Dude, I got it," she said, pointing to her temple.

"Ah, of course." He took a bite and studied her face. "What are you worried about then, if not Camael's well-being?"

She checked her phone. Still no text back. "Nothing."

He gave her a knowing squint and put his fork down.

"Fine. It's Will's girlfriend. She's not texting me back. She's a new vampire and I'm worried she's gone off and gotten herself killed."

"A vampire? Well, the apple doesn't fall far from the tree, does it?"

"She wasn't a vampire before he died."

"Well, that'll be a fun surprise, won't it?" he chuckled.

"Man, I hope Will's okay. I really don't want to have to send you to kill him again."

"You…you knew I was listening?"

"Of course I did."

He sat back and tilted his head. "So that Wyatt wouldn't blame you?"

She shrugged.

"How very manipulative of you. I'm impressed."

"I don't think B would see it that way, so shh."

"Your secret's safe with me."

"I told him about the party. He wasn't even mad. I forget sometimes how forgiving he is."

"Oh, *I* never do. You should have seen him after the Battle of Bravellir. He was sent to save King Herald, but the man all but begged to be allowed to die, thereby ensuring his legacy as a great warrior king, so I granted his wish. Barachiel was furious, but instead of giving me a lecture, he offered me a primitive form of jenever and sat with me while I complained. I was feeling particularly lonesome and--"

"I know all this."

"Then, how can you forget?"

"Because, man, I'm wrapped up in my own stupid shit a lot of the time. This human stuff is harder than it looks."

"Mm."

They finished their meals and Gabriel slid a credit card into the check presenter as the waiter scurried over to collect it. "Was everything to your liking?" the man asked.

"It was great," she told him.

"Yes, lovely, thank you," Lucifer said. The waiter nodded and walked off. "Tell me, sister. Do you think I'd be a good human?"

"No."

"You don't need to think about it a little?"

"Dude, do I have to remind you of the people in the church that time?"

"Do I have to remind *you* of the people in the theater that time?" he retorted.

"I didn't say *I* was good at being human. Shit, I might be more fucked up than *you*."

He raised an eyebrow and smirked.

She giggled. "Yeah, maybe not."

"Wendy!" Gabriel squealed, seeing her girlfriend sitting at the island as she and Lucifer entered the apartment. She darted over and kissed her repeatedly on the lips and cheeks. "I missed you so much. How was your trip?"

"Good. Hey, Lucifer. No bartender tonight?"

He glared at her.

"There's a lot to catch you up on."

"The bartender is no more, I'm afraid. Caught in Cain's revenge fantasy. Well, it's late. I'm off to bed." Lucifer headed down the hall. "See you in the morning."

"Night!" Gabriel sat next to her girlfriend, holding her hand and kissing it.

Wendy raised her eyebrows and pursed her lips. "What'd I miss?"

Chapter 7

Allydia used the key Wyatt had given her to enter his apartment and was horrified to find the Nephilim sitting casually on the sofa. She flew at him, baring her fangs and hissing. He jumped back in his seat as Wyatt stepped between them.

"It's okay," he told her, gently holding her back by the shoulders.

"It most certainly isn't. He's already killed you once. How is he even here? He should be rotting in the ground."

"Lucifer brought him back. I don't know the details and I don't care. What's important is that he's here."

She stared daggers at the boy, resisting the urge to lunge at him and tear his throat out with her teeth. "He's an abomination."

"What does that make you?" Will retorted.

"You have no idea what I am, the pain I will rain down on you if you so much as *breathe* on this man wrong."

"Relax," Wyatt said. "Nothing's gonna happen. We've been working on our meditation and--"

"*Meditation?*" she mocked. "Have you lost your mind? That boy is a menace. I give it a week, two at most before he's back to his monstrous ways."

"And, you'd know all about being a monster, wouldn't you?" Will snapped.

She glared at him. "I do what I do because I have to. I take no pleasure in hurting people. And, for the record, I haven't killed a human in years. Can you say the same?"

"Enough," Wyatt interrupted.

"She's got a point," Will conceded. "I don't know how long it'll be before I lose it again. Maybe I should stay with Aunt Gabriel for a while, just until we're sure I'm okay."

"That's hardly necessary."

"Let him go," Allydia begged.

"It's not that far and if I get out of control, Gabriel can stop me."

Wyatt folded his arms and furrowed his brow.

Will stood and patted his father's shoulder. "I don't want to hurt you, Dad."

Yo, B, he heard Gabriel say in his mind.

Yeah.

Michelle's not answering her phone. I called in a potential robbery to the house in Southport, but the cops said it's empty. Something's up.

"Allydia," he said, his tone accusatory as he met her gaze. "Do you know where Michelle is?"

"Michelle?" Will worried. "Dad, what's going on?"

Allydia frowned. "Don't ask me about this, Wyatt."

"Where?" he pressed.

"This is *my* business."

He closed the space between them, towering over her. She'd never seen him look so determined. "*Tell me*."

"Fine." She took a step back, feeling intimidated for the first time in centuries. "She's in the basement of the club, locked in a cell until I decide what to do with her."

"You put her in a cage?!" Will barked.

"She is not how you remember her."

"Let her go," Wyatt demanded.

"I can not. There are consequences to my actions. I have to consider--"

"Then, I'll get her myself." He pushed past her, Will following his father to the door.

"It is not your place," Allydia stated.

He turned back, looking furiously into her eyes, daring her with his words. "Stop me."

The men left, slamming the door behind them as the Queen composed herself, using her hand to fan her neck and chest. "Goddamn it, he's sexy."

Wyatt stormed through the club, his son at his heels. Vampires that recognized him from the battle in Iraq cleared a path, the fear in their expressions causing others to follow suit. At the back of the room, he spotted the door leading to the basement and quickened his pace, paying no attention to the hushed murmuring of the crowd around him.

"What are you doing here?" Hartley bleated, blocking his path.

"Get out of my way, Hartley," he commanded.

She arched an eyebrow. "Excuse me?"

"Step away from the lady," a half-drunk vampire said, coming up next to them.

Without altering his gaze, Wyatt shot a bolt of lightning into the man's chest, sending him reeling into a group of bystanders. "I don't want to hurt you, but you know I will." The Queen's assistant swallowed hard, pressing herself to the door behind her. Before she could decide whose punishment would be worse, his or her Queen's, she saw Allydia making her way toward them.

"Stop this now," she insisted.

He ignored his girlfriend's request, his eyes still fixed on Hartley's. *"Open the damn door."*

She looked to her Queen for instruction. She sighed and waved a hand, giving her the go-ahead, so she stepped aside. Will hurried past them, opening the door and bolting down the steps. Wyatt turned to address Allydia. "We need to talk." She gestured toward the steps leading upstairs, her annoyance clear in her expression. Before heading toward them, he stared daggers at Hartley as her hands trembled so hard, she nearly dropped her phone. "If anything happens to my son, I'll hold *you* responsible."

She slid back to her spot in front of the door, guarding it against further intruders as she watched the two go up to the second floor. She put her hand to her chest, glancing over to see the fallen vampire stand and take a glass of wine from a nearby table. "Well," she said under her breath. "That was dramatic."

Chapter 8

"Michelle?" Will called, his eyes adjusting to the darkness of the dungeon.

"Hello?" a weak voice called back. He dashed to it, finding the cell at the back of the room.

"Oh, God, Michelle," he breathed, stopping in front of the door. She was huddled in the corner, surrounded by empty blood bags, her hair disheveled, her dress torn, and her skin ashen.

She peered up at him, not believing her eyes. "Will?"

He gripped the bars and yanked the door off its hinges, flinging it aside and rushing in to kneel in front of her. He took her face in his hands, looking her over as she stared in wonder. "Are you okay? Are you hurt?"

She shook her head. "I'm fine. How are you here? Did I die again?"

Tears pooled in his eyes as he pushed the hair away from her face. "No. No, Lucifer brought me back. I don't know how or why, but...are you sure you're all right?"

She reached up and touched her fingertips to his chin. "You're real?"

"Yeah. Yeah, I'm real."

Her heart skipped in her chest as relief washed over. She kissed him hard, pulling herself up into his arms, almost knocking him over as she squeezed him. They embraced for several moments before Will stopped, tears of guilt tumbling down his cheeks.

"I'm so sorry," he whispered. "I never meant to hurt you."

"I know. I know you didn't." She ran her hand through his hair and down to his shoulder. "I can't tell you how much I've missed you. God, Will, I love you so much." She held him again, a swarm of butterflies fluttering in her stomach.

"I love you, too," he said, holding on to her like the last life preserver on the Titanic. "I feel like you're cutting me a lot of slack and I'm pretty sure I don't deserve it."

She laughed, kissing him again, softly at first, and then deeply, her body tingling as she pressed it against his. She pushed him down from his knees to a sitting position on the cool stone floor, positioning herself in his lap. She struggled to get his pants undone as she felt him stiffen beneath her, his hands running up her legs and under her dress. Just as she got the zipper unstuck, her fangs began to protrude, cutting his lip like a knife, the taste of his blood overwhelming her with lust and hunger. She leaped up, pushing him out of the way as she darted to the fridge across from the cell, threw the door open, and pulled out one blood bag after another, sucking down the contents, and dropping them to the floor.

He watched her, eyes wide as he gagged. "Oh, that's gross."

"You undermine me in front of my people," Allydia scolded as she and Wyatt entered her throne room, slamming the door behind them. "You attack them where they're meant to feel safe. *You disrespect me.*"

"You have a girl locked in a cage in an underground bunker. You don't get to be the one that's offended," he condescended, pacing around the room, hands on his hips, disgust in his eyes. "How could you do this?"

"I *had* to. There are *laws*."

"That *you* created! Look around." He gestured to the lavish throne at the other end of the room. "No one tells you what to do."

"I do what I must to keep my people safe."

"Safe? From what? What could they possibly be afraid of?"

"Each other!" she shouted. "You think me cruel and brutal, but I do what I do for a reason. They are not *human*, Wyatt. They are predators with appetites and emotions you can not understand. Without a firm hand to lead them--"

"Stop." He crossed his arms, rubbing one of them as if for comfort. He bit his lip as he looked at her, the anger and despair mingling in his features catching her off guard. "I've stayed out of your business. I ignored your past against my better judgement. But this? And what about Hattie? What did you do to *her*?"

She closed her eyes for a moment as she folded her arms and sighed, clearing her throat in defiance as she returned his gaze.

He let out a deep, sorrowful breath. "Right. Okay, I need to end this."

"This?"

"Us. It's too crazy. I can't have you anywhere near my son."

Her bottom lip quivered as she spoke. "You would leave me so coldly?"

"I don't want to. Even after this, I don't want to be without you, but you've given me no choice."

"There is always a choice. You choose me or you choose to abandon me. *Again*."

"I have to! I wish it could be different, believe me. You have no idea how much this is killing me. I love you, but I don't know what else to do."

She shifted her weight from one foot to the other as she struggled to maintain her composure. "That's the first time you've ever said that to me."

His features softened as he allowed his pain to show. He stepped forward, cupping her face in his hands and kissing her, a tear falling from his eye to her cheek. He slid his hands down to the sides of her neck as he rested his forehead on hers, breathing in the sweet scent of gardenia that hung in the air around her. "I'm sorry." He left the room, the Queen crumbling to the floor. She held her stomach as her mouth fell open in a silent scream.

"Your Majesty," Hartley yelped, hurrying in and dropping down next to her. She cradled her in her arms as she wailed, holding her head to her chest. She knew it wasn't her place to ask questions, so she didn't. Instead, she provided what comfort she could, being there for her Queen, as was her duty.

Chapter 9

Wyatt collapsed onto the couch, too broken to bother taking off his shoes. With Will and Michelle now safely at Gabriel's, he could finally deal with the emotions that had left him reeling, the events of the day swirling in his mind like a hurricane. He sat back, running a hand through his hair and breathing out slowly, tears welling in his eyes. "I did the right thing," he tried to convince himself. But, the quiet of the apartment weighed on him, his newfound loneliness crushing his chest like a discarded soda can. He wiped his face and turned his head sharply, thinking he'd seen something from the corner of his eye. He got up to investigate, checking all the rooms, but there was nothing. He went to the kitchen and got a bottle of water from the fridge, but as he turned the cap to open it, he was stopped in his tracks by a strange, familiar scent. He searched the place again, unable to locate a source, but he was sure of what he was smelling…lavender. "I'm losing it." He put the bottle down, took his phone from his pocket, found the number for his old therapist back in New Jersey, and hit 'call'.

"Yes," a sleepy voice answered. Wyatt looked at the clock on the oven and immediately felt guilty for not waiting until morning to make the call.

"Hi, Dr. Stratford. I'm sorry to be calling so late or…early. This is Wyatt Sinclair. I know it's been a while since my last session, but I was wondering if I could make an appointment for as soon as possible?"

"Mr. Sinclair? Yes, of course. Call Marjorie when the office opens at nine. I'll have her squeeze you into the first available. Is this an emergency? Are you having suicidal thoughts?"

"No. No, I just, um," He didn't know what to say. He wasn't even sure why he was calling. He couldn't exactly tell him the truth, that he just broke up with his vampire girlfriend because he was worried she'd kill his grown son who wasn't yet born three years ago when they'd last spoken, who died and was resurrected by Lucifer and that he was pretty sure he was now being haunted by his dead ex-wife. "It's been a weird day."

"Are you thinking of harming yourself or someone else?"

"No."

"Do you feel safe where you are?"

"Basically. Listen, I'm fine, I'm just upset and I'd like to talk."

"All right, Mr. Sinclair. Call the office in the morning and I'll see you soon."

He ended the call and put the phone on the counter, leaning against it and letting out a sigh of relief. He felt better just hearing the older man's voice, a sign to him that a visit to the psychiatrist was long overdue.

Gabriel finished hanging the blackout curtains in Wyatt's old bedroom while Michelle transferred blood bags from a medical cooler to a dorm fridge next to the nightstand. In the kitchen, Will organized the two hundred protein bars Gabriel had bought him by flavor in the pantry. She'd told him to wear cargo pants and always keep a few on him, just in case.

"William," Lucifer greeted as he entered the apartment. "Nice to see you. Gabriel tells me you'll be staying with us for a while lest you put your father in some sort of danger. What is my brother up to this evening? No doubt something scandalous with the vampire Queen."

Will shook his head. "He dumped her."

"You're kidding. I thought he'd moved past suicide attempts. Some things never change, I suppose."

"You said something like that earlier. What happened when I was gone?"

"Not my place to say."

"Like you care about decorum."

"Not generally, but contrary to what you may think of me, I do care about my brother and I'm quite certain he wouldn't want me burdening you with the events that took place in the days following your death."

Will formed a ball of electricity in his palm. "I can make you tell me."

Lucifer laughed. "I assure you, you can not."

"Fine." The lightning disappeared as he put his hands on the island, looking across to his uncle who sat on a stool, taking a peach from the bowl of fruit he'd insisted Gabriel buy. "Why'd you bring me back?"

"I have my reasons," Lucifer said, swallowing a mouthful of fruit.

"And those are?"

"Not your concern. I will say, though, that the look on your father's face when he realized you were back was worth all the effort." He stood and headed toward the hall. "Now, if you'll excuse me, it's late and I'm positively drained. I'll see you tomorrow. Oh, and William," He turned back, tossing the half-eaten peach into the trash. "Do keep in mind that should you again lose your way and bring any harm to my brother, I will tear out your heart and feed it to you before drowning you in the kitchen sink. Goodnight." He vanished into the room next to the one that would be Will's as Gabriel stepped into the hallway, rolling her eyes.

"Don't worry about him," she said, walking to the kitchen and taking a bag of chips from the pantry. She opened it and took one before tilting the bag toward her nephew. He grabbed a handful and sat.

"Why not? Would he not actually do it? Because that was really specific."

"Oh, he'd definitely do it. I just meant you shouldn't dwell on it. The chances of me letting you get that out of control again are pretty slim."

He almost choked as he swallowed his chips and reached for more. "You're threatening me, too? Not that I don't understand, but, *damn*."

"You know what you did, Will. I don't have to explain to you why we have concerns. *But*, I'm hoping that between me and Lucifer keeping an eye on you and your dad helping you with that meditation shit, this time will be different. And, if you start feeling rowdy, tell me this time, maybe, before you do something you can't take back. Okay?"

"Okay," he agreed.

"All right. I'm going to bed." She got up, leaving him the bag of chips, and walking toward her bedroom.

"Hey, do you think Allydia would hurt dad? Lucifer thinks--"

"Don't worry about it," she called back. "Your dad can take care of himself and if she tried anything, I'd fucking kill her."

"They asleep?" Michelle asked as Will came in, closing the door and setting a bottle of water on the nightstand.

"Yeah. A lot of death threats in this family. No wonder Dad took me to live somewhere else."

"I won't let anyone hurt you." She sat up on her knees on the bed, her tee-shirt, the only clothes she wore since her shower, just covering her backside.

"After what I did, I get it. They're right. I can't expect them to just be okay with me being here." His lip started to quiver as he spoke. "I don't know how you can still look at me without being scared or mad or *something*. How are you still looking at me like you love me?"

She held his face in her hands and looked deeply into his eyes, trying not to get lost in them. "I do love you. It broke me when Gabriel told me you were gone. *It broke me.* I know you wouldn't hurt me on purpose, even in that state. I know you, Will. You don't scare me. *You have me.*" She kissed him sweetly. "You have me." She kissed him again, pulling him down on top of her as she lay back onto the blanket.

His thoughts faded as he glided his hands up her thighs, pushing up her shirt, and squeezing her hips. She slipped out of her shirt entirely, then pulled his off, as well. He kicked off his pants and boxer briefs and ran his hand up her body, his lips moving from hers to her neck. She placed her hand on the small of his back as he sank into her, his lips brushing her neck as he breathed her in, the perfume of her like birthday cake and magic. The familiar, warm ache replaced all other feelings as he buried his face in her hair, letting her wash away his guilt and regret as she moved beneath him.

She clung to him like hope as the sound of his heavy breathing in her ear sent shivers through her body. Her gums throbbed as her fangs descended. She turned her head, trying and failing to escape the sweet smell of his skin and the blood just beneath it. She raised her fist to her mouth and bit down on it, sucking the blood from her own hand as a wave of euphoria flooded through her. Relief washed over her as she realized she could keep herself from harming him. She would never forgive herself if she bit him. He was back. Her only love was back and he was everything.

Chapter 10

Malik lay breathless in the dark, unable to sleep, his heart thumping in his chest. He couldn't get the image of his daughter's eyes flashing black and the threatening tone of her voice when she'd said she was hungry out of his head. He wanted to talk to his wife about his anxiety but was afraid she'd get angry. Sinclair was family and he knew how important that was to her. He knew that she loved him, but when it came down to it, her child would always be more important. Sinclair was her blood. He was an option. Still, he couldn't shake the feeling that something was off. He had to say something. He just had to be careful about how he went about it.

"Val," he whispered. "Valerie."

"Mmm."

"Val, wake up. I need to talk to you."

She opened one eye and glared at the clock. "Boy, it is five in the morning. I am not in the mood."

"No, Val. I really need to talk to you. Before Sinclair gets up."

She smacked her lips. "What is it?"

"I think something's off."

"What do you mean, 'off'?"

"When she came in here asking for eggs, her eyes turned *black*. Not like there was a shadow or something. Her pupils got *giant*."

"Okay."

"Okay? That's all you got to say?"

"Well, she's part vampire. It's bound to happen."

"What the-- how are you so calm about this?"

"Why are you in a tizzy right now? I told you what she was."

"Yeah, but--"

"She's a tiny child. What do you think is gonna happen?"

He gave her a knowing look.

"Boy, you're crazy. She is all right. Besides, you think Gabriel would leave her here if she thought she was dangerous?"

"Daddy?" a soft voice came from the doorway.

He cleared his throat and sat up. "Yeah, baby. Did you have a bad dream?"

"No." She came in and sat next to him on the edge of the bed, looking up at him with pleading eyes. "I just wanted to tell you you don't have to be afraid."

He swallowed the lump in his throat. "Afraid of what?"

"Me. I would never hurt you, Daddy. I promise."

"He knows that baby," Valerie told her. "Go back to bed. Sun's not even up yet."

"Okay, Mommy." She hopped down and pattered back to her room.

"See?" Valerie smiled. "She's fine. Now, go to sleep. I'm tired."

He lay back, clutching the comforter to his chest, his heart beating faster now than it had before he'd woken his wife.

Malik never slept. Instead, he got out of bed at six, made a big breakfast, and woke Valerie and Sinclair up with an idea he thought might help make things at least *seem* more normal.

"What do you say, after breakfast, we all go to the park?"

"YAY!" Sinclair exclaimed, jumping up from her seat and throwing her arms around his neck.

"I think that's a great idea," Valerie agreed.

"All right, eat up! There's a park a couple blocks away. We can walk there as soon as we're done."

"Thank you, Daddy!" Sinclair gleaned, shoveling bite after bite of pancake and hash brown into her mouth. Valerie flashed him an approving smile and the family finished eating, excited for the day ahead.

Sinclair held tightly to Malik's hand as they stepped onto the soft grass. The sounds of the other children playing happily made her smile from ear to ear. She couldn't wait to join them.

"Okay, I need you to stay where we can see you, right there on the playground. Don't go off into the woods over there. You could get lost."

"Okay, Daddy."

"Remember to be nice to the other kids and if you get scared or hurt, just yell. We'll be right here."

"Most importantly," Valerie said. "Have fun."

"I will! Bye, Mommy! Bye, Daddy!" She let go of her father's hand and skipped off, climbing up to the top of a slide and giggling all the way down. She had a blast, playing on the jungle gym and swings, hanging from the monkey bars, and sliding down the fireman's pole. She laughed to herself as she thought about her grandfather doing that countless times for work and wondered if it had been as fun for him as it was for her.

As her feet hit the bouncy pieces of recycled tires underneath the pole, she noticed a six-year-old boy sitting alone under a tree close to the edge of the forest. She walked over and sat on the ground in front of him. "Hi. I'm Sinclair. You wanna play?" He nodded shyly. She picked up a stick and drew a tic-tac-toe board in the dirt between them. They took turns holding the stick, drawing x's and o's until one of them won the game, scribbling them out, and starting over.

They played for about twenty minutes before the boy's father called from a bench, "Logan! Five more minutes, then it's time to go!"

"Look at that," Valerie said, gesturing to the kids. "She made a friend."

"I see," Malik said. "Maybe you were right."

"I was what? I'm sorry, can you say that again? I don't think I heard you."

He laughed and put his arm around her. *"You were right. She's perfectly fine. I overreacted. You happy?"*

"More than happy. I'm content." They shared a kiss and kept talking, taking their eyes off the kids just long enough for Sinclair to leave her new friend and have a quick chat with his father.

"Logan's daddy?" she asked the man who didn't look up from his phone.

"Mm-hmm."

"I saw the bruises on his arms. I know what you did. I'm asking you to stop it."

The man looked up from his screen and scanned the park to see if anyone had heard. Luckily, it looked like no one had. "Go away, little girl, before something bad happens to you."

Her expression turned stern as she stepped closer. "I asked nicely."

"Stay out of my business, kid."

Her hands became fists as she stared him down. She looked so serious and determined, unlike any four-year-old he'd ever seen. He almost laughed at her. Almost.

His hand flew to his chest as he felt a jolt followed by searing pain spread from his heart down his left arm. He panicked, unable to catch his breath.

"Don't put your hands on that boy again," she said through gritted teeth. "If you do, I'll know and you will *not* live to regret it, do you understand?"

His face went ghost white as he trembled, the pain in his chest unlike anything he'd ever felt. "What the fuck?" he choked as he slumped in his seat.

"You get it," she decided, skipping off and hugging her new friend goodbye. Just like that, the pain was gone. He gasped for air as sweat trickled down his temples, the color returning to his face.

"Aw," Valerie said as they turned back to see the children hugging. "How sweet is that?"

"Adorable," Malik agreed.

Behind the trees, the old woman watched, her long, spindly legs peeking out from her black, shapeless dress. Her wild, gray hair was largely unkempt, half piled up in a loose bun, unwashed, and attracting flies. She sniffed the air in the girl's direction, making sure to stay out of sight. She smelled the air again as the child rushed off to be with her parents. A crooked smile crept across the woman's face as she scratchily whispered, "Delicious."

Chapter 11

"Chocolate or fruity?" Gabriel asked, opening the pantry door.

"Fruity," Wendy said, sitting at the island. Gabriel took the red box from its spot on the shelf and opened it, pouring tiny, brightly colored flakes into two bowls before getting milk from the fridge. She poured the milk and got two spoons from a drawer, handing one to her girlfriend before sitting herself and taking a bite.

"That's hardly breakfast," Lucifer commented as he entered the kitchen.

"Hey," Gabriel picked up the box and pointed to the nutrition label. "It has eleven vitamins and minerals."

"Yes, well, clay contains iron, zinc, and calcium. I don't suggest eating that, either." He took a banana from the fruit bowl and went to the living room where he turned on the television and settled on the sofa to watch the last few minutes of the morning news.

Gabriel rolled her eyes as she took another bite. Wendy looked back to make sure Lucifer couldn't hear her before asking, "Is it weird that I find Satan endearing?"

She snickered. "Don't let him hear you call him 'Satan'. He hates that."

"Noted. Is it okay if I use your shower? I have a flight I'm already running late for."

"Again?" Gabriel complained. "I'm beginning to really resent your job."

"Just a day trip. I'll be back by dinner."

"Yeah, go ahead. What's mine is yours. And everyone else's, apparently."

"So, Will and his girlfriend got settled in okay?"

Gabriel shuddered, almost throwing up her cereal. "I don't want to think about it."

"Okay," Wendy chuckled. "Listen, before I go, there's something I've been meaning to tell you."

She put her spoon down and arched an eyebrow. "You got a side piece? Am *I* the side piece?"

She laughed. "No. Sometimes, when I go to work, I'm not just doing flight attendant stuff. Sometimes, I'm doing witch stuff."

"Witch stuff?"

"Like in New Zealand. No one called in sick. I went because there was a coven that needed help banishing an evil Earth Spirit. They were weak sauce. If I hadn't shown up--"

"You lied?"

"Yeah. Yeah, I didn't want to bother you while you were busy with that whole Cain thing. I figured you'd just worry and get distracted. I'm sorry. Are you mad?"

She chewed on her bottom lip. "I don't know. I've never felt like this before."

"Like what?"

Gabriel crossed her arms and thought for a moment before finding the right word. "Deceived."

"No one's ever lied to you before?"

"Of course, but I always *knew* they were lying and I always knew why. It didn't bother me. This is like, painful."

"I'm so sorry. I'll never lie again, I swear. I've just never told anyone about this. It was something my grandma always told me to keep to myself just in case."

"In case what?"

"Tituban magic is strong. In the wrong hands, it can be used to do all kinds of damage *if* it doesn't kill the witch trying to wield it first. If certain people knew who I was, really bad things could happen. I have to be careful. Please don't take this personally."

"Okay."

Wendy gobbled up the last of her cereal and kissed her cheek before rushing off to the bathroom.

Gabriel jumped up and threw her boots on. "Yo,"

"Hmm?" Lucifer acknowledged.

"Stay with the kids. I'm going out for a while."

He waved her off, never looking away from the TV. "Fine, fine."

She wasn't sure what to do with the strange emotions she was feeling. She was confused and in need of answers, so she decided to consult an expert.

"I need relationship advice." She burst in, swinging the door closed and planting herself at the kitchen island.

"So, you came *here*?" Wyatt asked.

"You were with the same chick forever. You kept a marriage going for *years* even though you were out of your mind most of the time, so, yes. I came here. Also, you're three blocks away and Uriel's in fucking Connecticut."

He shrugged and sat opposite her. "All right. What's up?"

"Wendy's been keeping stuff from me. Some side hustle where she goes off to who knows where to help other witches with their problems. How worried should I be about this? She *lied*."

"Well," he folded his hands. "Why'd she lie?"

"To protect herself from evil witches and to keep me from worrying, supposedly."

"You believe her?"

"I guess."

"I'd cut her some slack. You haven't been together long. She's probably not used to letting somebody in on her secrets. You might be the first person she's dated that knows she's a witch at all."

"Mm-hmm. Mm-hmm. *But, she lied.* She lied right to my face and I had no idea. Could say anything and I'd never know if it was true or not. How do I know she won't lie to me again?"

"You don't. You can't. It's the risk we all take to be with someone. I know you've never had to before, but if you want a relationship with her, you have to trust her."

"Trust," she pondered. "Interesting. Like faith."

"Exactly."

"Hmm."

"Crisis averted?"

"We'll see."

He leaned forward. "Can I ask *you* something?"

"Always."

He swallowed hard, not sure if he wanted to know the answer, but he had to ask. "You know everything about me."

"Yeah."

"Things I don't know about myself."

"Totes."

He took a deep breath. "Why do I love her?"

She tilted her head as her eyes softened. "You know why."

He shook his head.

"Because you're dumb."

He cast her an annoyed glare.

"Okay, serious now?"

"Please."

She cleared her throat. "It's a lot of things. You love her because she loves you. She puts you on a pedestal so high, you can't see the ground. You love her because you see her the way she was before. You see who she is underneath who she has to be. And, you love her because you need to."

He stared at her, his heart leaping to his throat. "I felt that in my bone marrow."

"You asked."

"You should be a therapist."

"Pfftt, like I have patience for that shit."

"I broke up with her," he lamented. "How do you think she's taking it?"

She gave him a knowing look. "Badly."

Chapter 12

"Thank you so much for coming," the girl said as she let Wendy into her dorm room. Her eye was black and swollen, her cheek bruised, and her lip split. "I didn't know who else to call. My mom said you helped people like us, even if we aren't practicing, so I--"

"First things first." She waved her hand over the twenty-year-old's face. "Pulchra."

"What was that?" She touched her eyelid and looked in the mirror above her desk, shocked at the transformation.

"No reason you should be reminded of what happened every time you look at yourself. It wasn't your fault, you know that, right? Some men are just trash." The girl nodded. "The glamour will hold until you've healed all the way. You have a picture?"

"Yeah." She took a photo from the desk drawer and handed it to her. "From Spring Break."

She tore it in half, discarding the girl's image so that only her abusive ex's face remained. She pressed it between her hands and closed her eyes while repeating the phrase, "Discede procul aeternum." After a few minutes, she opened her eyes. "You got a lighter?"

The girl hurried, rummaging through her drawers, finally finding a blue disposable lighter she'd used to light a joint the weekend before. She handed it over and Wendy lit the picture on fire, tossing it in the empty waste bin.

"Let that burn to ash. It'll put itself out when the spell's complete. Need anything else?"

She raised her eyebrows in shock. "No. Is that it?"

"Yeah, he won't bother you again. Remember, let that thing burn." She headed out the door.

"Thank you!" the girl called.

She waved. "Any time."

Back on the plane, Wendy couldn't help but feel guilty about keeping Gabriel in the dark about her extracurricular activities. After all, she'd trusted *her* with who *she* was. Angels, demons, vampires, all of it. Cain had spooked her, though. She could tell when she told her about him breaking into her place. She needed to focus and Wendy didn't want to be a distraction. Still, it had upset her to learn that she'd lied to her and she didn't want to be a source of pain for her new lover ever again. She'd make it up to her somehow.

Her phone buzzed in her pocket and she took it out, looking down at the screen and smiling. It was a text from the college girl thanking her again. She saw on her ex's social media accounts that he was packing up and moving to Japan. He didn't know why, he just felt like he needed to.

She laughed as she put the phone away and gazed out the window, the sky on fire with the sunset. She regretted not telling Gabriel about her work sooner, but she never once regretted the work itself. All her years of hiding who she was and all the time she'd spent practicing with her grandmother had been worth it. Helping witches who couldn't help themselves was her calling and she loved doing it. As much as being God's Messenger was a part of Gabriel, this was who Wendy was and who she'd always be.

Chapter 13

Allydia woke up on the floor, her assistant big-spooning her as the sun left the sky. She got up, waking Hartley as she smoothed her hair. She stood, glided to her throne, and sat, slinging one leg over the arm as the assistant scrambled to kneel before her.

"Good evening, Your Majesty," Hartley said, clearing her throat and adjusting her top.

"Good evening. I apologize for my outburst last night. You should never have seen me in that condition. Thank you for comforting me."

"Of course."

They were silent for a while as Allydia thought things over. Hartley kept her head bowed, her fingers laced behind her back, her gaze averted.

"I don't remember what freedom feels like," Allydia blurted, cutting the air with her words. "I'm not sure I've ever known it."

"Your Majesty?"

"I've spent thousands of years creating a kingdom, taking power for myself because I'd felt so helpless in my human life. I was little more than a servant to my father. He beat me, ridiculed me, showed me no mercy. Still, I stayed with him, even after I was married, so he wouldn't have to roam this world alone. He needed me. And, when my family was gone, I replaced them with all of you. Tell me, do you need me? Do any of you?"

"We love you, my Queen," she choked out.

"That's not what I asked."

Her bottom lip quivered as she dared to make eye contact. "We would, all of us, be dead if not for you. You saved us, not only from death but from our lives. You saved me from prejudice and judgement, bigotry, and hate. My own family cast me out. I died for being just a little of who I was and you gave me," She started to cry. "You gave me everything."

Allydia slid off her seat and onto her knees, wiping the tears from her assistant's cheeks, and searched her face. "Are you happy?"

"My Queen, I am a thousand times happier today than at any other time in my life and that is thanks to you."

She showed a whisper of a smile. "It was all worth it, then." She hugged her, putting her hand to the back of her head. She'd never shown Hartley physical affection like this before and the feeling of her Queen's arms around her was overwhelming. She slowly hugged her back, unable to swallow the lump in her throat. She sobbed into Allydia's shoulder, decades of repressed emotion pouring out in a waterfall of tears. "You're invaluable to me, Hartley. I'm so grateful for your presence in my life. Your family may have abandoned you, but I never will. No matter what happens, I want you to know that."

She pulled away and used her sleeve to clean the smudged mascara from her face. "I know that, Your Majesty." She caught a breath in her throat as she remembered what she'd been too afraid to ask about the night before.

"What is it?"

"I just thought I should ask, with the rebels wreaking havoc," She turned her head to listen for anyone near the door, not wanting the others to hear. There was no one. "Did Navid get home safely?"

Her eyes flashed. "How do you know that name?" She bolted up, Hartley too, standing on instinct.

"He was here, prowling. I sent him home. I didn't realize you had living rel--"

"Did you have him followed?"

"Of course, Your Majesty. Security was with him until he was safely on his flight."

She scowled, taking her phone from her pocket and calling his number. No answer. She stormed toward the door. "When the governors start to arrive, inform them that they are to stay here until I return."

"Where are you going, my Queen?"

"London."

She stood in Navid's apartment. Broken furniture and glass littered the floor while the stench of blood hung in the air like smog, thick and inescapable. Fury burned in her chest as she looked for clues as to who may have taken him, but there were none. The bakery she'd followed him to had been boarded up and abandoned. He was gone, no doubt a pawn in this 'King's' twisted game. But, if this unnamed vampire wanted to play, she would show him exactly who he was toying with.

Back at the club, the Governors began trickling in. Hartley got them up to speed and assigned them apartments on the third floor while she waited for further instructions.

"Hart?" a voice called. She turned in its direction and spotted a man she hadn't seen in decades. "It is you! You look unbelievable!"

"It's 'Hartley' now."

"I see that." He looked her up and down, a wide smile curling up his lips. "Seriously, you look *amazing*."

"You think so?" She couldn't help but flirt. Oliver had been an old flame, someone she'd dated back in the nineties. He'd attracted her right away with his Australian accent and chiseled features, but things fizzled, as they always did between her and other vampires. As much fun as she'd had with him, something never felt quite right. Her, probably.

"I do. You look...well, you look like you were always meant to."

She gave a proud smile, noticing how handsome he still was. "So, it's been a while. How have you been?"

"Busy. I opened a casino in Atlantic City."

"Finally! Congratulations. I know it was your dream."

"Yeah, it was. Still is. It's better than I could have hoped. People love throwing money away to forget their problems."

"That they do."

"So, I hear there's a pack of ruffians causing trouble."

"Something like that."

"Well, I'm sure the Queen has it under control. She's nothing if not capable."

Her phone rang and she held up her hand to excuse herself as she answered it. "Yes?"

"It's Phindi. I need to speak to Her Majesty at once."

"She isn't here. Can I help you with something?"

"You are loyal to the Queen, yes?"

"Of course."

"You can be trusted?"

"Yes, Genera-- I mean, *Duchess*. Your Grace. I am assistant to the Queen and I--"

"Yes, fine. I have information on the so-called 'King'. He's in Jordan. I've found his precise location and I need the Queen's permission to launch a full-scale attack. I have an army ready and waiting just out of his sight. And, there's something else. He's holding a man. A human. He's taken him prisoner and is keeping him hostage. I don't understand his reasoning for this, but the man has been given water and food. If he'd not been so badly beaten, I would think he was being kept as a pet."

Allydia appeared in a blur, snatching the phone from Hartley's hand. "Duchess Phindi, this is your Queen. Bring me the human alive. As for the 'King' and his sycophants, do what you must. Anything you have to. By sword, scythe, or sun, *kill them all*." She handed the phone back to her assistant. "Text me his exact location." Hartley nodded, the fire in the Queen's eyes sending a chill up her spine.

Allydia went to the center of the floor, her presence filling the room. "Attention." The music stopped. The lights went up. All eyes were on her. "As you may know, there are those among you that would see me overthrown. They call me 'distracted', 'weak', and 'unfit to lead'. If anyone here feels this way, I demand that you now come forward and state plainly that you oppose me." The crowd was silent, each vampire steady in their obedience to her. All, but five. She snuffed them out by the way their hands shook ever so slightly when she spoke and the grimaces they tried to hide. She moved faster than even they could see, plucking each one from the crowd, tearing their heads from their bodies with her bare hands, pulling hearts from chests and eyes from sockets, and piling up the parts at her feet for the others to see. "Anyone else?" she growled, licking blood from her palm. "Now is the time. With me or against, make your choice known."

The vampires bowed their heads, each taking a knee.

"Good." She turned her attention to Hartley. "Lock it down. If anyone threatens the faithful,"

"I will eviscerate them, my Queen."

She lowered her head. "Call everyone. Tell them to be ready for rebel attacks, even in the day. I'll handle the 'King' myself." She kicked a heart out of the way as she moved toward the door. "And get someone to clean this shit up."

Allydia cried as she washed the blood of the children that had forsaken her from her hands. Their betrayal was enough to cause her heartache, but what hurt more was the realization that this was the first shower she'd taken in her own apartment in weeks. She'd become accustomed to waking up and going to sleep at Wyatt's, his scent filling every room, his energy soothing. Now, just minutes before sunrise, she'd have to go to bed alone. Her stomach churned as she wept, covering her face with her hands under the scalding water. She knew that she was breaking, but she couldn't allow it. She had to rescue Navid and save her people. Only when that was done could she mourn. Only then could she decide how to proceed.

Chapter 14

Navid struggled with the shackles that dug into his wrists as he fought the dizziness that threatened to overtake him…again. He'd been in and out of consciousness since he'd been thrown in the cell, mostly due to the way he was being held there: by chains, upside down, hanging from the ceiling.

When he'd first arrived, vampires had swarmed him, stripping off his shirt and scratching his chest and back, licking his wounds as he tried to break free, all wanting a taste, every one of them gobsmacked by the familiarity they sensed in his blood. Some showed signs of trepidation while others laughed maniacally, savoring his flavor on their lips like a fine wine. Only when their leader, the one they called 'King', shooed them away did they leave him be. He'd brought him falafel, dates, and water, all of which he'd refused for fear of being poisoned. The food sat, untouched on the dusty floor and had begun to attract flies. He was drenched in sweat, dehydrated, and starving. His jaw ached from the gag in his mouth holding it open while muffling his angry screams. He growled in frustration as he tried to climb up the chain, hoping to release it from the hook on the ceiling, but his arms were too weak. Just when he thought he might pass out again, the cell door swung open.

"That's an unsettling shade of purple," the 'King' said, studying his face. "Toasted plum, I'd call it." With one hand, he unhooked the chain, dropping Navid hard on the floor. He winced as searing pain spread through his back and shoulders. He rolled to his side, facing his captor, wishing he had the fluid to waste by spitting on him, if only he weren't gagged. "You should eat, Navid." He knelt down and slid a new plate of food toward him which he batted away like a defiant cat. "Have it your way." He tucked his shoulder-length hair behind his ears as he looked down at his hostage, almost feeling sorry for him. "I'm not going to kill you. If I'd wanted to, I would have already and I wouldn't taint your food. I would just eat you. Do you know why you're here?"

He shook his head, though he had a pretty good idea. He'd heard bits and pieces of vampire chatter since he'd arrived, not to mention the blathering by Jack and Simon. This 'King' was staging a coup against Allydia and was using him as leverage. Didn't take a genius to figure it out. But, if he could keep him talking long enough, maybe the wooziness would subside and he could use his chains to strangle him and make a run for it. Not a solid plan, considering the place was overrun with vamps, but what choice did he have?

"You're here because it will infuriate the Queen. Nothing more, nothing less. When this is over, I *will* let you go."

He scrunched his eyebrows in confusion.

The King sighed. "You see, the Queen has always been feared. Respected. Beloved. That changed, however, when she all but disappeared for three years. She abandoned her people. Left them to their own devices. When she finally emerged from her sabbatical, she had the nerve to require their service in a war that was not their own. They fought and died in a battle for what? Do you know? Because none of us do. She rejects her own kind and instead takes a human lover and now we discover she has a living descendant. It seems that the Queen's priorities have shifted. Her people are simply learning to adapt to their new reality. They need someone new to lead them. They see me as their savior." He burst out laughing, causing Navid to jump in his skin. "*Me*. It's absurd. Do you not see the irony?" The bound man's expression told him that he didn't. "Oh, of course, you don't. Allow me to introduce myself properly. Some call me The Betrayer, a name earned yet still hurtful. My given name is Judas Iscariot."

Navid's eyes grew to saucers as his labored breathing quickened. His heart thudded against his chest and his mind raced. The gravity of what he was saying hit him like a ton of bricks. Could this be true? And, if it was, what did that mean? The implications were mind-blowing.

Judas turned his head to listen for eavesdroppers before addressing him again, his tone hushed. "The Queen's army marches as we speak. Most of my followers are here, awaiting battle. A few are scattered, awaiting orders. You'll be safe as long as you remain chained. The Queen has no intention of surrendering her crown. She is too proud. It is what I'm counting on. I have no interest in ruling over these foul creatures. My goal is the complete destruction of their kind."

Navid tilted his head, more confused than ever.

"Their gullibility and old-world misogyny make it easy to sew seeds of unrest. I control them like puppets on a string." He leaned in, twisted determination coloring his face, his voice dropping an octave. "I've barely lifted a finger in this fight. They were itching for war, so I've given them one. A civil war that will end this putrid empire once and for all."

Michelle crawled into bed, wrapping her arm around Will's waist and resting her head on his chest. He'd been asleep for hours, but as the sun began to make its ascension, she was just getting tired. His body was warm against her skin and the sound of his heartbeat was soothing, like a lullaby encouraging her to drift off. She listened to the air fill and escape his lungs, so grateful for the sound of it, she almost cried. As she began to fall asleep, she drew in a sharp breath, startled by the realization that she'd completely forgotten to tell him. She'd been so thrilled to have him back, it hadn't occurred to her that he should know. She had to tell him…now.

"Will," she whispered, sitting up and gently nudging him. "Will, wake up."

"Hmm?" He rubbed his eyes and sat up. "What time is it?"

"Six-thirty. I need to tell you something. Something important."

"Are you okay?"

"I'm fine, I'm just…a vampire."

"Are you hungry? You can drink if you want. It was kind of gross at first, but it doesn't bother me anymore. You have some bags left, right?"

"No, I'm not hungry, it's something else. I'm not sure how to say this, so I'm just gonna start at the beginning."

"All right." He took her hand, seeing how serious she was giving him a twinge of anxiety.

"After I turned, I went with the vampire that made me to her place in Scotland. We had to hide because if the Queen found out she'd sired someone without permission, she would have killed us both. I was hungry all the time. Like, more than normal. Hattie kept me in blood, but it was never enough. After a few weeks, it was clear why." She cleared her throat, stalling for time. "I started...showing."

He did a double-take. "You started *what*?"

"I was pregnant, Will."

His muscles tensed and his chin dropped. "You...how?"

"The morning after pill must not have worked. Maybe it was expired or something, I don't know. But, I was pregnant before I turned, so--"

He looked her over, putting his hand to her belly, the vacancy evident by the flatness of her abs. "But," His eyes shined with tears as he assumed the worst. "The baby died?"

"No," she told him, grabbing his hands and holding them to her heart. "No. Because of my weird vampire physiology or something and your Nephilim hyper-speed aging thing, she grew *fast*. Like, so fast, my ribs broke from the muscles underneath stretching out so quick. She didn't die, Will. She's fine. She's perfect."

"She?" Tears sprung from his eyes like water from a fountain.

"Her name's Sinclair, for you." She, too, began to cry. "I tried, but I couldn't keep her. I wanted to, you have no idea. When she looked up at me with your eyes," She stopped, choking back sobs as she tried to rein in her emotions. "But, I was afraid."

"Of what?"

"Of me. I was scared to death that I would," She covered her mouth, squeezing her eyes shut as the pain of missing her baby proved too great to contain.

"Okay," He held her close to him and settled back against the pillows. "It's okay. I understand." He kissed the top of her head and rubbed her arm. "It's early. You should sleep. We can talk about it tonight."

She sniffed, her eyelids feeling heavy. "Gabriel says she's okay, but I wish I could see for myself. But, I can't. I can't risk it. I would die if something happened to her because of me."

He lifted his head. "Gabriel?"

"Yeah, I gave her to your aunt. She's the only person I could trust."

"Mm. Okay, get some sleep." But she was out before he finished the sentence.

Chapter 15

"Where's my daughter?" Will exploded, causing Gabriel to choke on her banana.

"Boy, you are lucky Lucifer's still asleep. He can't know about her, yet. And, don't tell him I was eating fruit. I don't want to give him the satisfaction."

He threw a ball of lightning past her and into the kitchen wall. "Where?!"

"Yo!"

"Tell me or I'll--"

"You'll what?" She stood from her seat at the island and stepped toward him, arms crossed and eyebrows furrowed. "You're upset, confused, clearly pissed. But, don't forget who I am. God knows *I* never can."

"What'd you do with her?"

"I didn't hurt her. What kind of monster do you think I am?"

"The kind that would send a girl who should have been in college to spy on her nephew and kill him if she had to."

"She was never supposed to *kill* you. She was supposed to tell me if *I* needed to."

"I swear to Christ."

"She's with Uriel, your Aunt Valerie. She's fine, I swear. She made a friend at the park yesterday. Did him a favor. She's doing well. You don't have to be so grouchy. Eat something and settle the fuck down."

She went to the pantry, grabbed a box of granola bars, and tossed it to him. He tore it open, stripping a bar of its wrapper and gobbling it up in two big bites. He took another from the box and sat, his body finally beginning to relax.

She got a glass and filled it with milk, setting it in front of him and returning the jug to the fridge. "I would never hurt Sinclair," she promised, sitting across from him and taking a granola bar for herself. "She's different than you. She's in full control of her powers and her emotions and thoughts are always in check. I don't have to worry about her like I do you."

"Can I tell you something?"

"Any time."

He looked her in the eyes, hands trembling as he fumbled with another wrapper. "I'm worried about me, too."

Her eyes softened and she patted his hand. "You'll be okay."

"You don't know that. Look what I just did."

"Will,"

"The headaches are back. Not bad, but it's starting, just like before. When I'm with Michelle, I'm fine. I feel like me. But, any other time, it's like a bomb waiting to go off and the seconds are ticking down and I don't know how much time I have before--"

"Shut your mouth. Nothing's gonna happen, you hear me? I won't lose you again. Especially after what it did to," She stopped herself, taking a bite of her breakfast and looking down at the counter.

"What it did to who? To Dad?"

She looked back up and chewed, not wanting to answer.

"Lucifer wouldn't tell me, either, but it doesn't take a genius to figure it out. He tried to kill himself again, didn't he?"

She swallowed hard, knowing her brother had no intention of ever telling his son about what happened after he died. "I shouldn't tell you."

"But, he did, right? He tried? What'd he do? Slit his wrists? Pills like in college?"

"No. No, not pills."

"What, then?"

"Why are you asking about this? He's okay now."

"Because I'm back. But, if you have to--"

"No."

"But, if you do, I don't want him to fall apart."

"He didn't get better because you came back. He got better because," She dropped her granola bar at the sudden realization. "Because of her."

"Her? The vampire Queen?"

She nodded.

"She helped him? She actually cared about him?"

"Yeah, dude, she loves him. I've never felt love like that and I know everything everyone around me ever feels. Except you. And Wendy, which is nervous-making, I'm not gonna lie."

"I didn't know it was that serious. I mean, I thought I saw something in her eyes when she looked at him, but..." He swallowed another bite. "So, now she's gone, and if I have to die,"

"He'll feel alone again. *Shit*. Well, that's it. You can't die. Ever. You have to suck it the fuck up and figure out a way to control your shit because I will *not* lose my brother, do you understand?"

"Yes, ma'am," he muttered.

She folded her arms and bit her lip as she slowed her breathing, trying to get her heart to stop booming in her ears.

"I should go to Dad's."

"He's on his way to New Jersey. He'll be back in a few hours."

"What's he doing in New Jersey?"

"It's been some time, Mr. Sinclair. Tell me, what's spurred this sudden return to therapy?" Dr. Stratford sat with hands folded in his lap, his notebook and prescription pad at the ready on the table next to him.

"I broke up with my girlfriend and I'm not sure how I feel about it," he confessed, noticing how the small office seemed like a time capsule, not having changed a bit in the last few years. Even the doctor looked the same, the only difference being the frames of his glasses were black now instead of silver. "Her job is, um, demanding. There are things she does there that I don't, I don't know, approve of? I can't get past it."

"Hmm. I think I understand. Being the partner of someone that does sex work can invoke feelings of jealousy, inadequacy,"

"What? No, she's not a sex worker. She's...in charge of things. Policy-making and law enforcement. Sort of."

"Ah, so she works in government. I'm sorry. When you said 'approve', I just assumed. My own moral bias. I apologize. Continue."

"The point is, there are things about her that I hate. Things she's done. Things she continues to do. *I hate them.* But, I love her. Despite everything, I am completely in love with her. I'm in so deep, I can't see daylight. Literally, sometimes. It's like my heart and my head are on different pages. Different chapters. Different goddamn books altogether. My brain keeps telling me to stay away from her, but it *hurts*. I have physical pain in my *gut*. I crave her like food. I *need* her like a drug. It's not normal."

"That's an interesting word." He picked up the pen and jotted it down. "What do you think 'normal' is?"

"I don't know." He thought for a second, recalling the last time he'd ended a relationship. "When Annie left, I was sad. I felt lost. Discarded. Unimportant. This is something else. I'm not moping around and crying all day. I'm having a hard time breathing."

The therapist tapped his pen to his lips. "Perhaps, you're reacting to this breakup differently because you feel differently about this woman than you did your wife."

"You think I love her more than I did Annie?"

"I didn't say 'more'. I said 'differently'. Every relationship, romantic or otherwise, is different. Different dynamics, different personalities. For instance, last we spoke, Annie had suggested you get in-patient treatment for your hallucinations. How does this new woman feel about that?"

"I haven't had any since before I met her," he blurted, realizing immediately what a mistake that was.

"You haven't? How is that possible?"

He gulped, saying the only thing that came to mind. "My sister's a billionaire."

"Ah," he said, taking his glasses off and setting them on the table. "A sister? I don't believe you ever mentioned her before."

"I didn't know she existed until recently."

"Well, I see much has changed."

"Yeah."

"Listen, we could do a deep dive of why you feel the way you do and how you may or may not be able to reconcile your feelings for this woman with what you know to be true in your mind, but that could take weeks and I don't know when you'll get around to coming back, so I'll say this plainly. Take my advice: Always make decisions based on what your head tells you is right. Your heart is dumb as shit."

Wyatt erupted in laughter. "You cursed? I don't think I've ever heard you say 'shit' in my *life*." He held his stomach as he bellowed.

"Well, you're not the only one whose life has changed over the years. Do you remember that woman that interrupted our session a few years ago?"

He thought back to when he'd first met Gabriel right here in this office. "Yes."

"After some soul searching, I decided she was right. I *have* wasted my talents. In a few months, I'll be retiring to work on playing full time. I may never play Lincoln Center, but the piano is my passion. So, while it may be unprofessional, from now until I lock up the office for the last time, I'll use the words that drive the point home most effectively."

"Well, they sure did," he chuckled.

On the drive home, Wyatt thought about what the doctor had said, giving it careful consideration. He was probably right. His common sense was telling him to stay away. More than that, his instinct to protect his son demanded it. Still, he couldn't shake this feeling. It sat on his diaphragm like a boulder, radiating through him, begging him to change his mind and plead with her to come back to him.

I sent Will to your place, he heard his sister's voice in his head.

Is he okay?

He's fine. A little shaky. Michelle told him about Sinclair.

On my way.

Chapter 16

"Did you know?" Will asked as his father returned home.

He closed the door and dropped his keys on the island, sitting across from his son, three protein bar wrappers and a half-empty two-liter between them. "Yeah. I wanted to tell you, but it wasn't my place."

"For God's sake, what is it with you people thinking things are or aren't your place? If you know something that affects someone else, you should tell them."

"Michelle's her mother. She had the right to tell you herself."

He rolled his eyes.

"How do you feel about this? Three's kind of young to have a kid. Must be weird."

"Shut up," Will snickered, picking up a wrapper and throwing it at him.

He laughed.

"Gabriel said she's at Valerie's. She said she's happy there. Do you think that's true?"

"I think Gabriel would know if she wasn't."

"Yeah." He pursed his lips and rested his elbows on the counter, touching his linked fingers to his chin. "I'm really sorry, Dad."

"About what?"

"I don't know, man, pick something. Murder, property damage, making you a grandfather in your thirties, upsetting you so bad you tried to kill yourself."

"Who told you that? Lucifer?"

"Nobody had to tell me. It doesn't take a genius to figure out that the guy who attempted suicide a bunch of times because his dad was an ice cube would do it again when his inner angel killed his own son, although, I am one."

He arched an eyebrow and sighed. "Yes, you're a genius and I have some issues, but I'm all right. You don't have to worry about me."

"But, what if--"

"Let's go." He stood, picking up his keys and walking toward the door.

"Where?"

"To see my granddaughter."

"So, this is Will," Valerie said, ushering them inside.

"Yes, ma'am," Will replied.

"Did you just call me 'ma'am'? Sweetie, I know you think that's polite, but don't do that again."

Wyatt laughed.

"And you," she turned her attention to her brother, casting him a judgemental glare. "You need to visit more often. I know it's a trip, but I miss you."

"Grandpa!" Sinclair squealed from the top of the stairs.

Valerie grinned. "Speaking of people who miss you."

The child stepped carefully down the staircase and hurried to where they stood, holding her arms in the air for Wyatt to pick her up, which he did.

"Hey," he gleaned. "You got big."

"I know! You should have seen my dad's face. I thought he was gonna have an accident."

He laughed again, setting her feet on the floor. "Is he here?"

"No, he's at work," Valerie told him.

"Daddy!" Sinclair beamed as if noticing Will for the first time. She rushed over and hugged his leg. He froze, her warm reaction to him hitting him like water to the face. He hadn't expected her to know who he was. He thought there'd be an awkward introduction giving him time to get comfortable. But, she'd recognized him somehow and there was no stalling.

"Come see my room! My mom painted a whole wall with chalkboard paint." She took his hand and led him up the steps. He looked back to Wyatt who waved him on with a reassuring smile.

"See?" She pointed to the wall as they entered the room. It was covered in an elaborate scene: a sun in the top right corner, grass and flowers of various shades of pink and purple, and a rainbow stretching across a blue sky. "I can draw anything I want and when I want to draw something else, I can just erase it and start over. I made you something." She stood in front of a small table set low to the ground and took a piece of paper from the pile to her left. He knelt down as she handed it to him. "That's me, you, and Mommy," she pointed out. He looked down at the picture, impressed with how accurately she'd sketched them out with colored pencils, matching their skin tones and the color of their eyes perfectly.

"Good job, sweetie."

"Thanks. Can you give it to Mommy? I know she's afraid to come."

He tilted his head, surprised at how her words tugged at his heartstrings. "Yeah, I'll give it to her."

"Thanks, Daddy. It's okay, I understand. I know why she gave me away. She did the right thing. Can you tell her I miss her and I love her and I'm not mad?"

His eyes were pools as he nodded.

"Don't cry. I'm not sad. My mom and dad are really nice and now that you're back, you can come visit all the time."

"I will. All the time."

"Yay! You should go now, though. My dad's almost home and he'll feel threatened if he sees you here. It'll be awkward. He'll get better about it, though."

"Okay," he said, wiping away a stray tear. "I'll see you really soon."

She threw her arms around his neck and squeezed tight before whispering in his ear, "I know you're scared, but you don't have to be. Everything's gonna be okay, I promise. I love you, Daddy." She kissed his cheek and let him go.

"I love you, too, sweetie."

"I know."

Chapter 17

"Cake!" Gabriel cheered as Wendy opened the bakery box and presented it to her. Chocolate ribbons adorned the perimeter of the round layer cake while 'I'm sorry' was spelled out in vanilla cursive on the top. "You didn't have to do that."

"Yes, I did. I shouldn't have lied. Even if I could justify not saying anything about that part of my life before, lying about why I was going to New Zealand was really sucky of me. Oh, I almost forgot." She pulled a plastic container from her shoulder bag. "While I was there, I had these incredible meat pies. You have to try one." She removed the lid and handed her a pie before taking one for herself.

"You baked?"

"I'm multifaceted."

"Holy crap!" she said, mouth full.

"Right?"

"Lucifer, come taste this!"

He reluctantly got up from his spot on the sofa and joined them in the kitchen.

"It's real food like you like." Gabriel handed him a pie and took another bite of hers.

He gave it a sniff and took a bite, raising his eyebrows in approval and taking it with him back to the living room.

"Don't get crumbs on my couch!"

"I really am sorry about lying," Wendy said. "I've never been able to trust anyone with this before."

"Yeah, well, I've never had to trust anyone ever, which is something I need to work on, according to my brother."

Lucifer scoffed from the sofa. "You went to Barachiel for relationship advice? Are you mad?"

"Like *you* would have been a better choice." Gabriel retorted.

He shrugged. "Fair point."

"For the record," Wendy said, tucking Gabriel's hair behind her ear. "You've been a great girlfriend."

"Really?"

"Outstanding."

"Well, you are an excellent baker."

"Thank you. Maybe later, I'll show you some of my *other* talents."

"I'm pretty sure I've seen those."

"I still have some tricks up my sleeve."

Gabriel laughed.

"For the love of," Lucifer huffed, exasperated. "Can you two please take your incessant flirtations to a less common room? Some of us are trying to read in peace."

"Gladly." Gabriel flashed a devious smile as she walked toward her bedroom, beckoning Wendy to follow. "Bring the cake."

The old witch took the chicken bones from the pocket of her apron and arranged them in a circle in her palm. She turned them, one by one, as she uttered the incantation, "Otevřít dveře." In the apparent emptiness of the forest, a shimmering translucence appeared before her. She stepped through it, entering the unseen cottage, hidden to all but her. She replaced the bones and shuffled to the kitchen where a stew pot set simmering on the stove. She took the herbs she'd just picked from her apron and tossed them in, inhaling the aroma with her crooked nose. She picked up the large wooden spoon from the butcher block counter and gave the broth a stir, scraping up the bits that had stuck to the bottom while she was outside. An eyeball and two tiny fingers floated to the top as she tasted the hot liquid. She smacked her lips a few times and added a dash of salt, stirring it again before putting a lid on it and hobbling to the rocking chair just a few feet away in the living room. She sat, saving her energy. She'd need all she could muster when she finally went for the girl. She was almost out of food and the child from the park with the smokey eyes and the deadly abilities was powerful enough to fuel her existence for months if not years. From what she'd observed, she was sure once she got a taste of the girl's flesh, she'd be stronger than ever. She just had to get close.

As the sun set, Will waited anxiously for Michelle to wake up. He sat on the edge of the bed, holding the drawing their daughter had made for them, tearing up as he thought about what he'd say and how she'd react.

"Will," She opened her eyes and sat up. "Why are you sitting there like that? Is something wrong?"

"I just need to talk to you."

"Are you okay?"

"I'm fine. I went to see Sinclair today."

"What?" She stared at him, hope and worry in her eyes. "Is she all right?"

His lip quivered as he handed her the drawing. "She's perfect. She wanted me to give this to you. It's us."

Tears spilled down her cheeks as she studied the drawing. "How old is she now? She was just a baby."

"She's about four or five. She's aging a little faster than I did, but--"

"And she's okay? She's happy? Safe?"

"Yeah, she said Valerie and Malik are really nice. She said," he caught a breath in his throat. "She said she loves you and misses you and she understands why you gave her away. She said we can visit whenever we want."

She covered her mouth, stifling the cries that begged to escape her throat.

He took his phone from his pocket and showed her the picture he'd taken of her standing in front of the rainbow she'd created on her chalkboard wall. She looked down at the screen, sobbing into her hand. She closed her eyes, shoving the phone away, shaking as she wiped the tears from her face.

"I can never visit her."

"Of course you can," he told her. "She said--"

"It doesn't matter what she said, she's a kid. She doesn't understand what I am, what I could do to her. Besides, if another vampire sees me with her and figures out she's mine, they'll kill her. Not to mention, Lucifer. If you and your dad are hanging out, he won't care about where you're going. But, if I tag along? He might follow us just to make sure I don't try to eat you both."

"My dad wouldn't have to go with us."

"Yes, he would. I can't trust myself and I know in my soul that if I went feral, you wouldn't have the heart to stop me before I did something horrible. But, he would. Your dad would protect you and Sinclair with his life because that's what he does." She dropped her head, fighting back more tears. "I hate what I am. I hate everything about it. If you weren't back, I don't know how much longer I would've been able to hang on, Queen's dungeon or not."

"Hey," he lifted her chin. "You can do anything. You're amazing."

She smiled through fresh tears and kissed him softly before getting up and pulling on a pair of jeans. "I need to be alone for a while."

"Are you sure?"

"Yeah," She kissed him again and headed for the door. "I'm going for a walk. I'll be back soon."

He watched her go, wishing there was something he could do to make her feel better. As the pain in his head grew in intensity, he rubbed his temples and tried to focus on something else. He looked at Sinclair's picture on his phone, calming himself, taking a deep breath, grateful that she was safe where she was, away from Allydia and away from Lucifer.

Michelle wandered the streets for hours, ignoring the hunger growing within her, pushing it down, too overcome with emotion to worry about things as trivial as feeding. She swallowed her tears and concentrated on her steps, the sound her ballet flats made against the pavement, and the feeling of the night air turning crisper with the approaching Fall.

In the distance, she heard a woman scream. "Not your business," she told herself. But, as the stranger cried for help again, Michelle's instinct to help overpowered the one to self-preserve. She bolted toward the noise, deep into a wooded area of the park. There, she came upon a woman in leggings and a sports bra being dragged by the ponytail by a man twice her size. The two women locked eyes, the jogger's pleading for help as she fought to break free from the tall man's grasp. Without hesitation, Michelle threw herself at him, knocking him to the ground, forcing his hands away from his would-be victim.

"Run," Michelle warned the woman, who had already begun dialing nine-one-one. She hurried off just as the man sprung up and slapped Michelle across the face. She licked the blood from her lip, fangs descending, her pupils dilating. "That was dumb." She leaped up, striking him down with a back-handed smack. She flung herself on top of him, holding him down by the shoulders. Before she knew what she was doing, she clamped onto his carotid artery, draining him as he struggled beneath her, a fight no human could win.

When she'd had her fill, her mind cleared. She'd killed him. The guilt came immediately, hanging on her heart like a beehive on a thin branch, too heavy to withstand. She cried again, this time not because she missed her daughter, but because she missed herself.

Chapter 18

Phindi looked over her troops, more than two thousand strong, faces smeared in red paint to honor their Queen and flame lily petals covering their armor. They carried swords, machetes, and daggers, their bodies tense in anticipation of battle and their hearts set on revenge. They waited, somewhat impatiently, for the order from the general-turned-Duchess as she assessed the opposition that approached from less than fifteen thousand yards away. Most marched forward while others stood guard at the entrance to a narrow canyon. Beyond that, she knew, was where the so-called King was hiding.

She pounded her assegai on the desert floor as her soldiers stomped in unison, whooping and snarling, anxious to get to the fight. She lifted her spear and the crowd went quiet. She turned to face the oncoming enemy and shouted in her native tongue, "Iwa!"

They shot themselves as if from a cannon at the other side, piercing hearts and slicing off heads with relative ease. The enemy army wore no armor, instead donning the same green, hooded cloaks as the men that stormed her sanctuary. Though not a match for Phindi's trained soldiers, they outnumbered them three to one. It would take time, skill, and luck for her side to prevail. The King's men refused to back down, even as their numbers dwindled, death coming to them bloody and swift. Some seemed to carry no weapons and hurled themselves at the soldiers like cannon fodder, their skin burning as it touched the petals soaked in the sap of the flame lilies that Phindi had concentrated.

She plowed through the hooded men, butchering one after another as they came for her. It seemed too easy as the armies now became evenly numbered, Phindi losing five hundred or so soldiers to their forty-five-hundred dead. As she got closer to the entrance, she felt a sharp sting in her shoulder followed by a heat spreading through her arm. She turned her head to see herself bleeding from what looked like a bullet wound emitting a bright, white light. "UV bullets," she hissed, digging the projectile out of her flesh and crushing it in her fist. Shots rang out as the traitors opened fire, the Queen's army dropping like flies to the blood-stained sand. "Get the guns!" she ordered, flying through the crowd, chopping off hands and collecting the weapons more modern than her own and using them against their previous possessors. Her soldiers obeyed, attacking their enemies even in the face of death. Most were mowed down, but others were successful in their efforts, retrieving guns for themselves and slaughtering the hooded men that stood between them and the King.

In the end, every traitor was killed along with more than nineteen-hundred of Phildi's soldiers. Only eighty-six faithful remained, bloodied and bruised, but not broken. They made their way to the entrance, hell-bent on taking down the would-be King once and for all. But, as Phindi began to step through, a light flashed, filling the canyon and searing the exposed skin of her hand and arm. She yelped, jumping back, her face twisted in rage. "Take the cloaks!" she commanded, rushing to the corpse of a fallen traitor and stripping the body of its hood. She winced, recognizing the man as one of her own soldiers. He'd gone missing the day of the battle in Iraq. She'd assumed he'd been killed there. She never would have suspected him of being a turncoat. Her disappointment only fueled her anger as she covered herself and marched back to the canyon. A few of her soldiers beat her to it, though, eager to avenge their brothers and sisters, but even through the fabric of the cloaks, their blood boiled, their skin swelling and turning purple as they cooked from the inside out. Their screams echoed in the night as they perished faster than if they'd been standing in direct sunlight. Whatever was lighting up the canyon was far more powerful than anything Phindi had ever seen.

"What do we do now, Your Grace?" a soldier asked.

She thought for a moment, tapping her assegai on the ground, livid and disappointed in herself. "The only thing we can do. I will contact the Queen for further instructions."

Wyatt sat staring at the bottle of whiskey on his coffee table, alone, his chest heavy and his stomach in knots. No matter how hard he tried to convince himself that leaving Allydia had been the right thing to do, he couldn't get her out of his mind. The look on her face when he ended things, the quivering of her lip as he kissed her goodbye, and the smell of gardenia that lingered in the air crushed him and no amount of advice or therapy helped. He was lost for her and fighting the urge to run back to her and beg forgiveness was even more painful than missing her.

He rocked the bottle back and forth, his lips pursed, and his eyes slits as he fought to maintain control. A single tear slid down his cheek and he wiped it away, a low growl in his throat as he covered his mouth, his leg shaking.

Outside, Allydia watched, sorrow meeting concern as she cursed the glass between them, wishing with everything in her that she could be inside where she belonged. She belonged with him and she *would* find a way.

"Yes," she said, answering her phone. As she listened to Phindi's account of the battle in Jordan, fire replaced the emptiness in her gut. "I'm on my way."

"With respect, Your Majesty," Phindi said. "It is not safe. Even you won't survive this light weapon. How will you protect yourself?"

"I'm not coming alone." She ended the call and leaped down to the street, on her way to call in a favor.

Inside, Wyatt breathed a heavy sigh, standing from his seat and taking the bottle to the kitchen. He opened it and poured the contents into the sink, watching with a twinge of regret as it disappeared down the drain. He tossed the bottle in the trash and was suddenly smacked in the face by the overpowering scent of lavender. He slowly made his way back to the living room where there, sitting on the couch as if she owned it, was his dead wife's ghost. His heart skipped a beat as he caught his breath. She was beautiful, as stunning as the day they were married. His eyes pooled as she turned to look at him, a kind smile on her soft pink lips.

"Come sit with me," she said, her voice like a song in his ears. He did as he was told, unable to take his eyes off of her, her skin glowing, her hair like gold. "How are you, really?"

"I-I don't know. Sad, I guess. Stressed. Worried."

"About what?"

Tears fell as his face remained still. "Will. He doesn't think I see it, but I know he's feeling shaky. I'm afraid of what he'll do and I'm scared that I'll," he swallowed a lump in his throat as more tears trailed down his cheeks.

"You don't have to worry about Will," she told him. "He'll be just fine, I promise."

"How can you know that?"

"Where I am, there's no such thing as not knowing."

"Then why'd you ask how I was?"

"Because you needed to say it out loud. Now, tell me about the vampire."

"Are you sure? That seems kind of inappropriate."

She laughed. "Maybe, but you need to work out your feelings before something bad happens. I don't want to see you up here for a long long time. So, spill. What's the dilemma?"

"She's a murderer that threatened our son's life. She had his girlfriend in a cage in a dungeon."

"True, but she loves you."

He wiped more tears from his face. "That doesn't matter."

"Of course it does. She can make her threats all day, but she would never lay a hand on Will. She knows you'd never forgive her if she did. She is head over heels. She loves you as much as I do and trust me, that's a lot. She will never hurt Will or you. As far as her being a murderer, that's horrible and it might take some effort for you to look past it, but for your sanity, you should really consider it."

"You're serious?"

"I know you, Wyatt. You need her. She keeps you from falling apart."

"You're not wrong about that," he conceded. "I'm sorry. I'm so sorry, baby. I had no idea--"

"I know. It's okay. Dying wasn't the best time I've ever had, but holding Will and looking down into that sweet baby's face was well worth it. I have no regrets. Now, I have to go, but I want you to promise me that you'll take care of yourself."

He took a shaky breath. "I promise."

"And, Wyatt, I want you to know this, I mean *really* know it. What happened to me wasn't your fault."

He nodded.

"You're a good dad, Wyatt. I'm sorry I ran away without telling you you were gonna be one. I should have trusted you. *You* should trust yourself now. Do what's in your heart." She blew him a kiss and faded, disappearing, the scent of lavender scrubbed from the air.

He fell back in his seat, wiping away the remaining tears, his head spinning. "Do what's in my heart." He sat up, resting his elbows on his knees, covering his face, and screaming into his hands.

Chapter 19

It had been hours and Michelle was still not back from her walk. Will paced the floor of the living room as the others slept, his head pounding and his blood pressure climbing. His mind raced with worry as his heart drummed in his ears. He looked again at the picture of his daughter on his phone, hoping the image would calm him. Instead, it triggered a borage of intrusive thoughts and paranoid delusions. His brain filled with images of her being hurt, beaten, and drowned all at the hands of his devilish uncle. He tried to shake them, telling himself they weren't real, that Lucifer had no idea she existed. But, the visions kept coming, flashing in his mind in bits and pieces, eventually replacing all logic with a rabid sense of urgency. His breathing quickened and his steps became deliberate, taking him swiftly to his uncle's bedroom.

He threw the door open and pounced, leaping onto the bed and wrapping his hands around Lucifer's throat.

"What mischief is this?" he choked, but as he grabbed his nephew's arms to pull them away, white-hot electricity flowed through them causing him to seize, the skin of his neck crackling like bacon.

"I won't let you hurt her!" Will screamed, his eyes wild, his cheeks red. "I'll kill you before I let you anywhere near her!"

Foam dribbled from Lucifer's mouth as he shook. Finally, he was able to push the boy off, but he came right back, punching him in the jaw with electrified fists.

"Damn it, Will!" Gabriel yelled, using her telekinesis to toss him to the floor. He stood, moving like a predator back to the bed. She waved her hand, pushing him back against the wall and holding him there. "The fuck's your problem?"

"He's rambling on about me doing harm to his girlfriend as if I have any interest in that." Lucifer healed, getting out of bed and cracking his neck. "While I do find vampires generally to be vile and ridiculous creatures, she seems perfectly--"

Will broke free of Gabriel's hold and jumped onto the bed, balls of lightning at the ready as he fixed his gaze on his stunned uncle.

"Somnus," they heard from the hall. Will collapsed, unconscious, his head hitting the pillow as if it belonged there. They turned to see Wendy, arms folded, shaking her head. "The violence in this family, I swear. You should really work on just loving each other. You okay?"

"No worse for the wear. If you'll excuse me, I'm feeling a bit peckish." He moved past them and went to the kitchen.

"And, you?"

Gabriel bit her lip, placed her hands on her hips, and took a deep breath. "Not really."

"What was that all about?"

"He's losing it...again. I don't know what to do."

"Yes, you do," Will said, sitting up, light-headed and groggy.

Wendy's mouth fell open. "How are you awake?"

Gabriel sighed. "He's special."

"Lucifer should have left me where I was." He sat on the edge of the bed and rubbed his temple.

"Shut your hole."

"You know I'm right." His shoulders slumped, the rage gone from his now somber face.

"Boy,"

"You know what I'll do. It'll be Lucifer, then you, then whoever walks through that door next. Dad. Michelle. You see what I am. You have to kill me."

"What the hell?" Wendy snapped.

"I'll get in the tub myself. All you have to do is hold me under if I try to fight it." He got up, looking his aunt in the eye, tears starting to form in his. "I can't control what's going on in my head. You have to stop me before I do something that can't be undone."

Gabriel took a shaky breath, fighting back tears of her own as she wrapped her arms around him, hugging him tight and smoothing the back of his hair.

"Tell them I'm sorry."

She nodded.

"Look out for Dad."

"Of course."

"Damn," Wendy blurted. "It is not that deep."

They turned to look at her, still lurking in the doorway. Gabriel wiped the tears from her cheeks. "You don't understand."

"No, I get it. Can't control his powers, they're making him crazy. He's dangerous, blah, blah. It's nothing a little self-control spell can't fix."

Their mouths hung open. He stepped closer to her, studying her face for signs of deception. "Are you serious?"

"Yeah. Give me like, forty-five minutes to gather up the ingredients. Try not to kill anyone in the meantime." She hurried to the front door and left the apartment leaving the two awestruck and staring at each other in disbelief.

"Can she really do that?" Will wondered. "Can she fix me?"

"I don't know. I guess we'll find out."

"All right." She sat on the floor of Gabriel's living room and took the supplies from her bag. She spread out a six-by-six green cloth and spilled a handful of garden soil in the center. Next, she placed a lace agate in the dirt followed by a nugget of frankincense. Then, she sprinkled a pinch of motherwort and took a sip of water, not wanting her throat to go dry as she recited the incantation.

"Are you sure this'll work?" Gabriel asked.

"Leave her alone," Lucifer lectured from the sofa. "Tituban witches have been pulling off miracles for centuries. No reason to doubt this one now."

"Don't worry," Wendy smiled. "I got this." She rubbed her hands together and began the spell. "Earth within and Earth below, teach him what he needs to know. Not so quick to flare or flow, but like stone both strong and slow." She bundled up the cloth around the other ingredients and tied it with a black thread before tossing it to Will who sat mesmerized across from her. "Go put that under your bed and never move it. When you wake up tomorrow, you'll be all better."

"That's it?"

"Yep."

He got up and went to his room, shoving the parcel under his bed against the wall directly underneath the middle of the headboard.

"That's really all it takes?" Gabriel asked.

"Yeah."

"Well, damn, no wonder you're the witch community's on-call fixer."

She giggled, getting up and heading to the kitchen to wash her hands.

"Did you see that shit?"

"Mm-hmm," Lucifer acknowledged, not looking up from his book.

"You think it'll work?"

"I assume so."

"Why aren't you more excited?"

"I'm ecstatic. Thrilled beyond words. Jumping out of my skin."

"Dude,"

He rolled his eyes and put his book down. "I'm very happy that our previously savage nephew will soon be in complete control of his faculties. I'm just also tired and still slightly aggravated by his latest outburst."

She gasped, clutching her hand to her stomach.

"What is it?"

"Barachiel," she whispered, not wanting Will to hear. "He's in trouble."

Chapter 20

Wyatt was awoken by the sound of his front door being kicked open. He flew out of bed, already gathering energy as he went to the living room to see who'd broken in. Before him stood a dozen male vampires, fangs exposed in twisted grins as they eyed him like steak, licking their lips, nearly panting at the sight of him. One stepped forward, drool leaking to his chin. "You do look tasty. I guess that's what she sees in you."

"What do you want?"

"Dinner."

He looked over the group, taking note of their positions in the room.

"You're the one the bitch Queen chose over us. We were forsaken for *you, a human*."

"Not just human," he corrected, forming a ball of electricity and eyeing the lumbering brute. "I was *going* to give you a chance to change your mind, but then you had to go and be disrespectful. *No one* calls my girl a bitch." He threw a bolt of lightning into the vampire's chest, sending him flying into the wall on the other side of the room.

"You do not scare us with your parlor tricks, Lightning Bearer," one of them hissed. "You may be strong, but we are many." They attacked, surrounding him in a sea of fangs and maniacal laughter. He fought them off, using all the energy he could handle to throw bolts and balls of lightning in all directions. The air sizzled and snapped, every hair on his body standing on end.

Yo, B, what's wrong? He heard Gabriel ask.

Angry vampire hoard.

I got you. Hold up your hand like you want to answer a question in class.

He did, using his free hand to punch a vampire in the nose, breaking the bone and knocking him out cold. He turned to the sound of a window breaking and was puzzled by the sight of a wooden mallet flying toward him. He caught it and on instinct whipped it back, driving a hole through the forehead of a vampire trying to sneak up behind him. He spun around, facing the raging beasts as they came for him. He lunged at them, one after another, bashing heads in, cloaked in a field of electricity. Every vampire that got close was sent reeling, falling to the floor in a seizing heap. He crushed their skulls with the hammer, taking out his pent-up aggression on his attackers, leaving none standing.

His chest heaved as he caught his breath, the bodies strewn in a bloody mess on the hardwood.

Do you need us to come help? Gabriel asked.

No, I'm fine. It's over.

From the corner of the room, he heard a low gurgling, the grumblings of a dying man.

"You're not dead?" he asked, approaching the one who'd insulted Allydia. He was slumped against the wall, bleeding from the head, his stomach burned and smoking.

He coughed, his arms too weak to cover his mouth. "It will not be that easy to kill me, human."

He crouched in front of him. "So, you're telling me this rebellion Allydia was talking about is because of *me*?"

He spat blood on the floor. "You don't know? She left us *for years* to pine for you. She is derelict in her duty. She had an obligation to *us*. But you charmed her away so we must follow another."

"Another?"

He laughed before coughing again. "We do as our King commands and soon, he will tear your whore Queen into pieces. He will slaughter that cun--"

Wyatt drove the handle of the mallet into the vampire's heart, unwilling to listen to anymore. Blood spurted from the creature's mouth as the light faded from his eyes. His head fell forward, his life extinguished. Wyatt stood, letting out a sigh of relief as he walked through the bodies to the sofa. He dropped onto it, suddenly aware of how tired he was not just physically, but emotionally. He was exhausted, sick and tired of denying himself what he needed. Annie was right. He needed Allydia, but how could he rationalize being with her?

He'd have to give it some serious thought, just as soon as he cleaned up this mess.

"What kind of trouble?" Lucifer asked for the third time.

"He's fine now," Gabriel told him, walking toward the door to let Allydia in. She opened it, startling the vampire who hadn't yet knocked. She quickly composed herself, clearing her throat and coming inside.

"We had an agreement."

"I know."

"The price for my aid in your Father's war was the deliverance of my descendants."

Gabriel crossed her arms. "And, I delivered them to you."

"Navid is in danger, held captive, no doubt afraid for his life. You *will* do as I ask."

"I shouldn't get involved."

"Hey, Allydia," Wendy said as she exited the bathroom.

"Hello."

"You okay?"

"No."

"This isn't my business," Gabriel told her.

"Be that as it may," Allydia seethed. "I require your assistance."

"Dia,"

"Messenger."

"It isn't my place."

"As if any of you care to stay out of the affairs of others."

"Girl, you had that child in a cage. What did you think he would--"

"Don't change the subject. We are talking about Navid. He's been kidnapped by a deluded psychopath and I need your help in freeing him. I do not ask for help easily, but I do it now because it is necessary."

"Who's Navid?" Wendy asked.

Allydia tapped her fingers on the counter. "My grandson."

Gabriel rolled her eyes. "One hundred and eighty-second great-grandson. You're barely related at all."

"You have a living relative?" Lucifer asked. "Does he share your penchant for mild stalking?"

Allydia glared at him. "Yes, actually."

"Don't chime in," Gabriel told him.

"You're really not gonna help her?" Wendy shamed.

"It's vampire business and it's all the way in Jordan."

"It's her kid, kind of. If you can help, you should."

She sighed. "Well, if you're gonna guilt me into it. Fine, but only because he had his goons attack Barachiel earlier."

Panic flashed in Allydia's eyes.

"He's fine." She shifted her gaze to Lucifer. "Just in case more show up, though,"

"On my way." He rushed out the door just as Michelle was coming in.

"Will!" the girl yelled, terrified of what the Queen would do to her. He stumbled out of the bedroom, half-asleep and rubbing his eyes.

"You're back," he said, giving her a peck on the lips. She pointed towards Allydia who cast them an annoyed glance before addressing Gabriel again.

"Let's go. It reeks of immaturity in here."

Gabriel snickered and kissed Wendy on the cheek. "Can you stay with the kids?"

"Of course."

"We're not children," Will said. "We don't need a babysitter."

Gabriel smacked her lips. "She's a baby vampire and you're three."

Allydia did her best to hide her amusement as she and Gabriel walked past them to leave. Gabriel stopped in front of her nephew and grabbed his face with one hand.

"How do you feel?"

"Well, my cheeks hurt a little, but fine, otherwise."

She laughed, letting go. "How's your head?"

"Great. I think it worked."

"You're welcome," Wendy called.

"Thank you," he chuckled.

"Okay, be good," Gabriel instructed. "I'll be back by this time tomorrow. Get some sleep. Love you."

"Love you, too." As Gabriel left, Will and Michelle retreated to their bedroom.

"What are you thanking the witch for?" Michelle asked.

He sat on the bed and took a protein bar from the nightstand. "She did a spell to help me stay calm. I should be in full control of myself now."

"You were slipping again?"

"Oh, yeah. Big time. I almost killed Lucifer. I got it in my head that he was gonna kill Sinclair. I could see him doing it like it was happening right in front of me like it was real. Oh, there's a pouch of rocks and dirt under the bed. Wendy said to leave it there for the spell. How was your walk?"

She wanted to shelter him from the events of the evening, to allow him the happiness she could see all over his face as he'd told her about his night. After a few seconds, she simply said, "Dark."

Chapter 21

"Well, this is a fine mess," Lucifer commented as he entered his brother's apartment, taking note of the blood-soaked paper towels that littered the floor.

"Yeah," Wyatt said, sweeping glass into a dustbin. "I never would have thought shoving corpses in an incinerator would be an average Wednesday night for me, but here we are. Gabriel send you to check on me?"

"Just a precaution."

"Mm-hmm."

"So, you'll be pleased to know that your progeny has been cured of his affliction."

He stopped what he was doing. "What?"

"Our sister's witch worked a spell calming his mind and giving him control over his powers and temper."

"You're telling me he's...normal?"

"Aside from the ability to put on a rather impressive light show and an immeasurable capacity to retain knowledge, yes. Good thing, too. I overheard him practically begging Gabriel to put him out of his misery."

He dropped the broom. "Why would he do that?"

"He gave himself a fright trying to kill me."

"He tried to kill you?"

"Like father like son."

"What did you do?"

"Nothing, I was fast asleep. The boy convinced himself I was plotting to murder his girlfriend. Before you ask, I wasn't."

"Is that why you're here instead of Gabriel? She didn't trust you two alone together?"

"No, she's off to Jordan with the vampire Queen to rescue her much-removed grandson from something or other, I wasn't really listening. You'll be interested to know that when Gabriel mentioned you being attacked, your beloved showed signs of concern."

He raised an eyebrow.

"I thought so."

"I think I made a mistake."

"Of course you did. I'm surprised she didn't order the attack herself."

"She's angry?"

"No," Lucifer considered. "She seemed to be in mourning. I'd venture to guess that if you wanted her back, you could have her. If she doesn't get herself killed in the meantime."

He picked up the broom and leaned it against the wall. "Did I thank you for bringing Will back?"

"You didn't need to."

"Thank you. Seriously."

"It was nothing."

"It wasn't nothing. It was huge. I almost regret kicking your ass when I thought it was you that killed him."

"Almost?"

He laughed and brought him in for a hug, patting his back a few times before letting him go.

"All right, that's enough affection. You're clearly exhausted. Go to bed. I'll finish cleaning this up."

"Really?" Wyatt asked.

"Yes, yes. You've earned it, what with avoiding being quartered by creatures of the night and all."

He laughed again. "Okay, thanks. Goodnight."

"Goodnight."

Wyatt disappeared into his bedroom while Lucifer swept more glass into the bin. He smiled to himself, his brother's gratitude like a warm hand over his heart. He would never admit it, but Barachiel's approval meant a lot to him, in human form or otherwise.

As the sun began to rise, the last of the guests finally went to bed. Governors and diplomats had apartments on the third floor while everyone else slept on cots in the cellar. It wasn't ideal, but if the traitors infiltrated the club during the day, it would look empty to them at first glance. Since no one usually spent the day there, it would be reasonable for the rebels to assume the building was empty and go, leaving the slumbering vampires alive and oblivious to the fact that they were ever there at all.

Hartley made one last lap around the building ensuring all locks were locked, her UV gun strapped to her hip just in case. She planned to sleep with it on the nightstand in the Queen's personal quarters, wanting to be close enough to hear if there were any intruders. When she was sure the building was secure, she headed up to the throne room where she found Oliver waiting for her, shirtless with a bottle of rum.

"What are you doing?" she giggled.

"I remembered rum is your favorite as is my chest."

She laughed out loud. "This is the Queen's throne room. We can't do this here."

"What about in there?" He tilted his head toward the bedroom.

"We shouldn't. It would be highly inappropriate."

"Come on, she doesn't have to know."

"Oliver,"

"When I saw you downstairs, I thought you looked like a snack. When I realized who you were, I had to have you. Tell me you don't want me and I'll go. Do you want me to go?"

"No, I don't," she gleaned. "And, I'm not a *snack*. I'm a fucking buffet because I'm a lot and you're never really sure where to start." She turned her head and ran a painted fingernail down the side of her neck. "I suggest right here."

"As you wish," he said, tossing the bottle into the throne and nibbling at her neck, wrapping his huge arms around her slender frame. She laughed again as he lifted her up and carried her to the bed. He kissed her hard as he removed the rest of his clothing before flipping her over and sliding her pants off. He kissed the back of her neck while he got a bit of lotion from the bedside table and smoothed it over himself. She gasped as he slowly entered her, lifting her hips and reaching around to caress the only part left of her that was still male. She covered her mouth, muffling her cries of pleasure, feeling it necessary to be as quiet as possible as to not wake the others. She gripped the headboard, steadying herself on her knees as all thoughts of the danger they were in left her mind.

When they were done, they fell asleep there in the Queen's bed, tangled up in each other's arms, too spent to bother covering themselves.

Chapter 22

"Sorry about that whole trying-to-murder-you-in-your-sleep thing," Will said, refilling his uncle's cup with coffee.

"That's all right, William. We all have days where we feel particularly homicidal. Besides, the feast you've made has more than made up for it. I've been living on take-out for months. Your aunt keeps nothing of substance in her kitchen aside from a carton of orange juice that I'm fairly certain expired last year."

"You could go shopping, cook for yourself."

He squinted and shook his head. "That sounds rather dull."

"Morning," Wyatt said, emerging from his bedroom.

"Hey, Dad. I made breakfast. Sit down, I'll get you a plate." Will took a plate from the cabinet and piled it high with two pancakes, scrambled eggs, bacon, and mixed berries. He set it in front of his father before pouring him a cup of coffee.

"Your son's quite the chef, Barachiel," Lucifer complimented, taking a sip of coffee and placing his cup back on the counter. "I don't think I've eaten so much since The Field of the Cloth of Gold."

Will thought for a second. "June, fifteen-twenty."

"Yes. You know your history."

"I know a lot of things."

He stood, taking one more sip from his cup before putting it down for the final time. "Very good. Well, I'm off. I called someone about fixing your window. They should be here momentarily."

"You didn't have to do that," Wyatt said.

Lucifer patted his back. "I don't *have* to do anything. But, it needs to be attended to. Wouldn't want a bird to fly in, would we?" He headed toward the door.

"Bye," Wyatt called.

He waved without looking back and left the apartment.

"He's not as bad as I thought he'd be," Will said.

"He has his moments."

"He told me about the vampires. You okay?"

"I'm fine. Speaking of vampires,"

"Michelle wouldn't hurt a fly."

"I'm not talking about her, although, I feel like I should tell you to be careful."

"Allydia, then?"

He nodded, taking a bite of his pancakes. "God, I missed these."

"You want to get back with her?"

"I don't think 'want' is a strong enough word."

"You know what I'm gonna say, right?"

"That she's a monster and a murderer and I should run away screaming?"

Will laughed. "I think you figured that out on your own. No, I was gonna say you should do whatever you want. You don't have to ask my permission."

"I wasn't."

"No, you were just gauging how I'd feel about it before making a decision that would inevitably be whatever you thought I'd be most comfortable with. You're still doing it."

"Doing what?"

"Putting everyone else first. Listen, Dad, you don't have to worry about me. I almost killed *Lucifer* last night. Gabriel couldn't even stop me. Wendy had to knock me out with some magic word."

"She's done that to me, too. Best sleep of my life."

"For me, too, for thirty seconds. She told me it should've kept me under for eight hours. I'm stronger than all of you. And, now that I'm able to control myself, there's no reason for you to be concerned. Your girlfriend can't hurt me. More importantly, you deserve to be happy. If the Queen of all vampires is what you need to live your best life, go get her."

"My best life?" he chuckled.

"Dad,"

"Okay, you're right. I was putting your feelings first. I probably always will and not just because that's who I am as a person. You're my kid. I have to consider--"

"I'm not a kid. I *have* a kid."

"You're three."

"I wish you'd all stop saying that. You know I'm like, twenty-seven."

"Yeah, well, I was changing your diapers three years ago."

"That's really gross."

"You have no idea."

"So, are you gonna call her?"

"Lucifer said she's in Jordan. I'll find her when she gets back. I probably have some serious groveling to do. This is the second time I've bailed. Should talk to her in person."

"Mm."

"There's something I should tell you."

Will took a bite of bacon from his third plate of the morning and looked up with raised eyebrows.

"Your mom stopped by."

He choked. After a few coughs, he took a gulp of milk and put his glass down. "What?"

"She said she loves us and she has no regrets. Seeing you in the hospital is her favorite memory. She's happy she had you."

Will's eyes were huge. "But, she's...I don't understand."

"She was a ghost."

"Oh."

"She went back to Heaven."

"Okay."

They sat in awkward silence as they finished their breakfast. As Wyatt took his last sip of coffee, a pigeon burst in through the broken window, panic-flying around the living room, knocking over a lamp. He put his cup down and sighed. "Damn it."

Chapter 23

"That's a lot of exploded vampires," Gabriel said, turning up her nose at the thousands of corpses that littered the desert floor. Even in the dark of night, it was a disgusting scene.

"We buried our dead before the sun rose," Phindi explained. "But the traitors did not deserve that kindness."

"All right, but someone is bound to see this."

"You will burn the bodies when we leave," Allydia told Gabriel, her impatience clear in her tone causing Phindi's stomach to flip.

"Apologies, Your Majesty. I should have disposed of the rebels' bodies. I let my emotions get the best of me. It will not happen again."

"It's fine, Duchess."

"Again, I apologize, my Queen. I have failed. I could not deliver the man who calls himself King to you. I can not get through the tunnel of ultraviolet light."

Gabriel stepped forward, rolling her eyes as she walked toward the canyon. "I can." She got to the entrance, pulled her sunglasses down over her eyes, and stepped inside. Along the eighty-mile-high cliffs were hundreds of spotlights filling the narrow passage with so much UV light, Gabriel's skin was beginning to darken. "Death by tanning bed." She went back to the group. "Hope you guys don't mind walking over broken glass." She held her hands in front of her and closed her eyes. After a few seconds, the lights shattered, raining down glass so loudly, the vampires had to cover their ears. Finally, it was dark.

Phindi held back a smile as she looked to her Queen for approval.

"If you find the hostage before I do, bring him to me *alive*."

"Yes, Your Majesty."

Allydia nodded, stepping aside to make way for what was left of her army to begin their assault. Gabriel stood behind her, in no mood to get trampled.

"For the Queen!" Phindi shouted, raising her assegai.

"For the Queen!" the rest cheered. They flew through the canyon, all but ignoring the cuts they got on their legs as they moved through the two feet of glass.

Gabriel stood next to Allydia and folded her arms. "I feel like they could have just thrown rocks at them and accomplished the same thing without dragging me all the way here."

The Queen arched an eyebrow.

"Your boy's in a cell. Take the stairs on the right when you first get inside."

She looked at her with a puzzled expression.

"I can hear his thoughts. He's scared. And dehydrated. You should hurry."

She spun on her heel and bolted into the canyon. Gabriel tilted her head as she heard something familiar. "Is that? *No way.*" She chuckled as she, too, slowly made her way into the canyon.

On the other end of the passageway was a large courtyard now flooded with battling vampires. The faithful sliced, shot and hacked their way through a force triple their size, slaughtering the lot of them while taking massive casualties of their own. Allydia barreled through, ripping out the throats of any hood-wearer in her path. She reached the massive door flanked by two Roman columns built into the side of the mountain. Without hesitation, she stormed inside, locating the staircase Gabriel had described and making a beeline for it. Not far behind, Gabriel entered the building, having snuck past the fighting vampires who seemed to have no interest in what she was doing there.

Downstairs, Navid clung to life by his fingernails, lying on the floor, his lips chapped, and his breathing shallow. Judas had removed his gag to attempt to feed him, but he wouldn't accept food. He didn't want to risk being poisoned or fed vampire blood. As he felt himself slip away, he began to regret that decision.

"Navid!" Allydia gasped, rushing to open the cell door.

"A-All," He couldn't form the words. His throat was too dry.

"It's all right," she told him, breaking the shackles from his wrists and ankles. "You'll be all right." But, as she was about to help him to his feet to leave, six rebel vampires slammed the cell door shut with Allydia and Navid still inside. They cackled as they gloated in their apparent victory.

"Not so big and bad are you now, *Your Majesty*," one mocked.

"When your friends outside are dealt with, we'll be back," another threatened. "Maybe show you what you're missing, being with that human lightning rod of yours instead of your own kind."

"I think you've forgotten to whom you're speaking," she said.

"We know exactly who you are, bitch, and we'll be back for you." He grabbed his genitals and stuck his tongue out while the others laughed.

She knelt down and whispered in her grandson's ear, "Close your eyes. I don't want you to see me this way."

He nodded and squeezed his eyes shut as she stood, sauntering to the door, never taking her eyes off the vulgar traitor. With one powerful kick, she knocked the door off its hinges and into the men standing behind it. In a blur, she plunged her hand into their chests, pulling their hearts from their bodies as they fell, the dumb looks of shock on their faces with them now for eternity. She used one of their cloaks to wipe the blood from her skin before turning back to the cell. Seeing it up close, she noticed the small palm leaves embroidered on the deep green fabric. It would have been beautiful had it not been worn by such a treasonous sycophant.

She helped Navid up, putting his arm around her shoulder as he stood. He opened his eyes to see the mutilated corpses on the ground and was so grateful to be free, it didn't occur to him to be frightened of the long-lost relative that had saved him.

In the makeshift throne room at the center of the building, Gabriel couldn't help but laugh. "Judas? Oh, my Christmas. It's been *forever*."

"And, who might you be?" he asked sitting in the stone seat perched on a small platform a few steps above the rest of the floor.

"It's me, Gabriel. It's okay that you don't recognize me, new body and everything."

"Messenger?" He stood from his seat and stepped down to meet her. "It *has* been some time. What are you doing here?"

"Not sure, to be honest with you. I try to stay out of politics. It's not my place to interfere in this kind of stuff, you know? Besides, Dia could've handled this on her own. All I did was turn off a light, which I maintain could have been done without me. But, you pissed me off, so, here I am."

"You misunderstand my motives, Angel. I don't seek power for myself. I want to destroy the vampiric race once and for all. It's what I was meant to do, to live long enough to make amends for what I did."

"No, I get it. Still dumb as shit."

"How have I offended thee? I have no quarrel with you."

"No, you *want* no quarrel with me, but you fell ass-backward into one. I would have stayed out of it, but you put my brother in danger. That was unwise."

"Your brother?" He stepped back, stroking his beard as he came to the realization. "The Lightning Wielder? He's an angel?"

"Obvs. What did you think he was?"

He shrugged. "Wizard. Warlock. Street magician. So, the Queen's taken up with an angel. Amazing. If I may ask, which angel is he?"

"The best one," Allydia said, entering the room, nearly carrying an exhausted Navid with her.

Gabriel hurried to them, helping Navid sit on the floor before taking a bottle of water from her bag and opening it, holding it to his lips. She placed her other hand on his back, healing the cuts that covered his torso. After a few sips of water, he took the bottle from her and looked her over, eyes wide with wonder. She took her hand away as he looked down at himself and back at her.

"Gabriel," she introduced herself. "Messenger of God, archangel, yappaby shmappaby. We should get you on the plane into some air conditioning. I have snacks. Chips, cupcakes, cookies." They stood and she began leading him away. "We'll get you some real food when we land. Some steak, maybe?" He looked back at Allydia with concern. "She's coming. This'll just take her like, a second."

When they were gone, Allydia rushed Judas, gripping his throat and throwing him down into his throne. He didn't fight back. Instead, he laughed.

"It's too late, Your Majesty. By now, they're dead, all of them. I have won."

She fumed, her whole body trembling with rage. "I should have forced your maker to kill you when you slaughtered that village."

He scoffed. "I killed my maker *before* I butchered that village. I was tricked into becoming one of you. I wanted him to pay for what he did to me."

"I took pity on you. When I found you alone in that inn, I showed you mercy."

"You shouldn't have."

She screamed, pounding her fist into his chest, breaking his ribs. She tore open his shirt and clawed at his flesh, peeling back the skin and muscle and prying open his chest. She reached into the cavity and plucked out his heart, holding it before him.

He smiled and in a voice barely audible even to her, he gurgled, "I am redeemed."

Outside, Gabriel cleared a path, waving her hand at the mess of glass in the canyon and leading Navid through. Phindi and a handful of faithful were all that remained of the vampires, the rest broken and battered in lifeless heaps on the blood-soaked sand.

"Messenger," Allydia called as she exited the building. Gabriel turned, stopping as the Queen approached her, her soldiers at her heels. Stern and stoic, Allydia gave her command. "Burn it all." Gabriel nodded and the group exited the canyon, stepping around the bodies that peppered the landscape. When they were clear, Gabriel flicked her wrist, igniting the corpses within and without. Navid's eyes grew wide as he watched the flames over his shoulder, the stench of the smoke wafting through the night air turning his stomach.

The battle was over, but at what cost? Allydia was heartbroken, her entire life feeling like a waste.

Phindi and her soldiers headed back to Egypt in disgrace, unable to make eye contact with their disappointed Queen.

Chapter 24

Hartley woke to the smell of smoke. She tried to turn the bedside lamp on, but it didn't light. The power had been shut off. In the distance, screams echoed through the club, snapping her to attention. She jumped up, throwing her clothes on and smacking Oliver on the back. "Wake up!"

"What?" He sat up, rubbing his eyes. "Is it still day?"

"I don't know, but there's a fire. Get your sexy ass up. We have to go."

He quickly complied, getting into his clothes and following her out of the room, through the throne room, and into the VIP area. The smoke was thick, but even through the dark haze, Hartley could make out several hooded figures holding closed the door to the basement. "Hey!" she shouted down to them before opening fire, hitting each one in the head with UV bullets, their treasonous bodies falling with thuds to the floor. She leaped down over the railing while Oliver hurried down the steps. She rushed to the door, kicking the rebels out of her way and opening it up, getting punched in the face by the heat of billowing smoke. She fell back as Oliver met her, both horrified as a man on fire tumbled from the cellar door and fell, no more than a giant lump of smoldering charcoal.

"The diplomats," Oliver breathed, bolting back to the staircase and following it up to the third floor, Hartley close behind. But, as they reached the landing, they were stopped in their tracks by an all-consuming wall of fire.

"Do you hear that?" Hartley shuddered.

"What? I don't hear anything."

"Exactly. The screaming stopped." They exchanged terrified, knowing glances before turning to race down the steps. Halfway to the bottom, the staircase gave out, dropping them down in a pile of rubble. They clawed their way out and headed to the door, opening it just enough to see if sunlight would meet them should they exit. Light poured in and they slammed the door back. Hartley made a beeline for the dead rebels and tore two of their cloaks away. She raced back to the door and handed one to Oliver. They covered themselves and stumbled out onto the sidewalk, a firetruck already pulling up in front of them. They retreated to an alley and hid there, neither of them sure how to answer questions about how the fire started or who had shot the men whose bodies had not yet burned.

"Are you all right?" Oliver asked, looking her over.

"Yeah. You?"

"Could be worse, I reckon."

She took her phone from her pocket and began dialing.

"Who are you calling?"

She held the phone to her ear and cleared her throat. "Everyone."

Navid slept across the aisle, an empty bag of cheese puffs still in his hand, while Allydia sulked.

"I'm sorry about your people," Gabriel said, sitting in front of her.

"Are you?"

"Well, I'm sorry you're sad."

"That's something, I suppose."

"I know this is a bad time, and I know you're not thinking about it, but I'm also familiar with you, so it needs to be said."

She cast her a look of derision. "What?"

"I don't want to be a dick, but you know what I'll do to you if you hurt my brother, right?"

She leaned back and rolled her eyes. "It is your brother that inflicts pain."

She gave her a confused stare. "Did you forget who he is? Protector of Humanity. He might not care much about *himself* most of the time, but his kid? You mess with Will's shit and all that Barachiel instinct comes flooding to the surface like a fucking dam broke."

"The boy is a menace."

"Wendy fixed him. He's fine now."

She raised an eyebrow. "Really?"

"Mm-hmm. I didn't think it was possible, but that bitch has *skills*." She looked over at Navid and back at her. "I mean, come on. Look what you just did for Navid. A hundred and eighty-two generations removed *and* you just met. Imagine if it had been Fatima, Naima, Sada, or Thaddea."

"You invoke the names of my daughters?"

"And imagine if, on top of all that maternal instinct, your sole purpose for existing was to protect people. To save them. It was who you were on your deepest level. If the tables were turned, how would you have reacted? What wouldn't you sacrifice for your children?"

She glanced over at her sleeping grandson and back at Gabriel. "He sacrificed nothing. He's disgusted by me. Afraid."

"Bitch, he is *broken in half*. He came to *me* looking for answers. *Me*. Do you know how fucked up a person has to be to--"

"I saw him struggling. I didn't dare hope that his melancholy was for me."

"Girl, with the stalking. For real."

"So, the Nephilim is under control?"

"Looks like. He did almost kill Lucifer first, though. It was hilarious. I mean, horrible and upsetting, but the look on Lucifer's face when I couldn't hold Will back," She laughed. "Ah, I wish I'd gotten a picture."

"You're sure he poses no threat to Wyatt?"

She nodded.

"Interesting."

Navid woke up coughing and Allydia went to sit next to him, handing him a water bottle and rubbing his back. He took a drink and looked up, his eyes fixed to Gabriel.

"Uh, oh," she said.

"What?" Allydia asked.

"He's star-struck."

"You're Gabriel?" he asked. "As in, Muhammed's first revelation?"

"Sort of."

"You met him?"

"Yeah."

His jaw dropped.

"Dude, get it together."

"I'm sorry, it's just...you're the most beautiful thing I've ever seen."

"She has a girlfriend," Allydia discouraged.

"I don't mean like that. I mean, that too, but, well, you're a bloody angel! A creature of divinity. Love and light and all that."

Gabriel crossed her arms and shook her head. "You need a nap."

He drew in a sharp breath as he suddenly felt ashamed of his lack of respect. "I'm so sorry." He slid off his seat and onto his knees, putting his head down in reverence.

"Oh, dude, no. No, don't do that."

"I'm sorry, I don't know what the appropriate thing to do is."

"*Not that*. Makes me wildly uncomfortable. I'm not *God*. Plus, I'm pretty much human right now, so." She waved her hand dismissively and he got back in his seat.

"You can understand his reaction, Messenger," Allydia warned. "You will treat him with kindness."

Navid looked shocked. "Are you threatening an angel?"

"She's also sleeping with one," Gabriel chimed.

Allydia scowled.

"What?"

"You're what?!" he gasped.

"It's not your concern," she said, handing him a bag of chips. "You should eat something else."

"He was gonna find out," Gabriel defended.

He opened the bag. "That's allowed?"

"It's not *not* allowed."

"My head is spinnin'."

"Eat," Allydia instructed, "Then go back to sleep. We'll be home in a few hours. You'll stay with me until I'm sure no one's left to harm you." She went back to her seat across from Gabriel as Navid ate, staring at the two women in front of him in amazement. "So," she said, turning her attention back to the angel. "Tell me about Lucifer's face when he thought his life was in danger."

Navid choked. "Lucifer?!"

Chapter 25

The old witch hid in the trees, watching for the girl with the power of death. Days had passed and she was beginning to lose hope. Finally, as if by answered prayer, the child returned, her parents helping her across the monkey bars. She looked older somehow as if she'd aged a year. She'd have to act fast. If the girl aged into double digits, she'd be of no use to her. Her patience wearing thin and her stomach grumbling, she followed the family to their house, creeping behind the fence as they entered the backyard.

Malik prepped the grill for the last barbecue of the season while Sinclair played in her sandbox and Valerie went inside to get the meat. Suddenly, the gate flew open, and the croan burst through.

"Baba Yaga!" Sinclair cried, pointing to the old woman.

"Baba what?" Malik asked as he stepped in front of her. "The hell do you want?"

"The child," she hissed. "I *need* the child."

"Lady, you best--"

She whacked him in the face with her cane made from an old broom handle, splitting his lip. She thumped him again, in the head and then in the stomach.

"Mommy!" Sinclair screeched.

Valerie looked out the kitchen window and saw the old lady beating her husband with a stick. "The fuck?" she muttered.

With Malik on the ground, the wind knocked out of him, Valerie hurried to get her sword from the top of the hall closet, running out to the yard as the witch approached Sinclair.

"Bitch, you best get the fuck off my property!"

"The mother," the woman bemoaned. She ran at her, bringing the cane down hard against Valerie's blade. They sparred, exchanging blows, neither wavering for a second. Sinclair sprang up, trying to make a break for it.

"Uh, uh, pretty," the witch crooned, bringing her hand up, causing the sand to rise and swirl around her in a tornado of filth.

"Oh, it's like *that*? Okay, I see you." Valerie cracked her neck, the sword erupting in flame. The witch stepped back, her shock quickly dissolving as her desperation forced her to continue. She slammed her cane into the sword again, but after a few strikes, the wood charred and ignited. She dropped it and curled her fingers toward the ground, lifting a large chunk of earth up, breaking it free from the rest. But, before she could raise it high enough to threaten the angel, Malik leaped up, snatched the sword from his wife's hands, and drove it deep into the old croan's chest. Her clothes caught flame and she screamed, her whole body going up in a plume of embers and ash. The ground returned and the sand fell, freeing Sinclair.

"Daddy!" she yelped, running into her father's arms as he knelt down, hugging her tight.

"Are you okay?" he fretted.

She nodded, a wide smile spreading across her face.

"I love you so much," he told her, fighting back tears. "I love you so so much."

She giggled. "I know."

Allydia stood in the rubble of what used to be her club. Oliver sat on the sidewalk, head in hands, as Hartley updated the Queen.

"The delegation from Norway was en route when the attacks occurred, so they're safe. They landed just after sunset. Governors from the Philippines and Nepal are also secure. I sent them to a hotel on Madison and 50th. Phindi and her group are in Alexandria and the Governor of Paris has barricaded himself in his chalet and refuses to leave. Everyone else is," She took a beat, placing her hand over her heart.

"And the rebels?" Allydia asked.

"Dead."

"You're sure?"

"Yes, Your Majesty. The ones that didn't die in the attacks were dealt with by my humans. I left none alive, I assure you."

"How many of us are left?"

She choked back her tears. "Twenty-nine, including us."

"Total?"

She nodded. "Their attacks were coordinated, Your Majesty. Small groups of traitors infiltrated every one of our homes and businesses simultaneously. They all but wiped us out." She brushed away the tears she could no longer fight.

Allydia appeared cold, even as her heart sank. "Transfer ten million dollars from my personal accounts to each survivor, including yourself. Contact the insurance company. Rebuild the club as you see fit. Make it a sanctuary for our people. Keep them safe."

She looked puzzled. "Forgive me, my Queen, but this sounds like goodbye."

"What did I promise you after you stayed with me the night that Wyatt broke my heart?"

"You said you'd never abandon me," she said, her lip quivering.

"And I never will. So, this is not goodbye. Do you trust me?"

"Of course, my Queen."

"Good. I will see you again, have no doubt." She cupped her face in her hands. "Until that time, stay strong, have faith in your capabilities, and be happy."

She nodded, stifling more tears.

"Good to see you alive, Oliver."

He stood and bowed his head. "And you, Your Majesty."

"I trust your casino is insured."

"Yes, Your Majesty."

"Perhaps I'll visit it once you've made any necessary repairs."

"I would be honored, Your Majesty."

"I have some business to attend to," she said, turning to go. "Take care of each other."

Chapter 26

Navid sat at Allydia's dining table, still drowsy and starving. Gabriel opened the takeout containers of steak, mashed potatoes, haricot verts, and yeast rolls, and handed him a plastic knife and fork. She took a bite of bread and picked up her own fork, casting him an annoyed glare. "You're staring."

"Sorry, I just can't believe I'm on a date with an angel."

"Not a date."

"No, I know, but, you know what I mean."

"I'm just here until Dia gets back to make sure you don't get kidnapped or eaten."

"Yeah, I know, but I'm freakin' out, right? How am I supposed to behave around you?"

"Dude, just eat."

"Should I call you 'Messenger' like Allydia does? Or would you prefer the full 'Messenger of God'?"

"My name's Gabriel."

"Right, but--"

"Bro, it would be way less annoying for me if you'd just treat me like a normal person."

"All right, but I don't know if I can."

"Give it a shot."

"I'll do my best." He took a bite of potatoes and glanced around the room. "Why does she even have a table?"

"Appearances."

"Right."

"Your dad's in Edinburgh, by the way."

He coughed up a bit of bread. "What?"

"He's a curator at the national museum there. After college, he took a trip to Scotland and fell in love with it. He's been there ever since."

"How…"

"I know things."

"Ah."

"I'm telling you this because you have a deep-seated desire for family. I'm not saying you shouldn't spend time with Dia. She loves you like a son. I'm just saying, she's not the only game in town."

"You're sayin' I've got a dad in the UK, not eight hours from where I live?"

She took a sip of soda. "Mm-hmm."

"And, you know this because of your angel powers or whatever?"

"Yep."

"Well, I'll be damned."

"Nah, you're good."

"What's he like?"

"Uh, tall, swarthy, fifty. Smart. Still kind of a man-whore, never settled down. Plays the violin. Still drinks a lot of wine."

"I don't know what to say."

She shrugged, taking a bite of potatoes.

He cut into his steak, unable to take his eyes off her.

"Dude, stop staring."

"Right, sorry." He lowered his head and took a bite, his gaze still fixed on her.

"Dude!"

Navid is safe now. Meet me at your apartment, Allydia texted to Gabriel as she stood outside the door. She knocked, ready to swallow her pride.

"Allydia Cain, as I live and breathe," Lucifer greeted, stepping aside to let her in.

"Where's the boy?"

"Asleep, I'm afraid. Is there something I can help you with?"

"No." She sat at the island. "I was hoping to make amends."

He sat across from her. "Oh, I wouldn't worry about that. Young William isn't the type to hold grudges, unlike your father. Did you know he murdered the woman I was seeing recently because of what happened between us in Akrotiri?"

"No, I didn't. My condolences."

"And, mine to you on the loss of your father."

"Unnecessary, but thank you."

"I did have a bit of fun torturing him before Wrath did him in. I would apologize, but you know better than anyone how badly he deserved it."

"I do. I almost hurt him myself after he told Wyatt to leave me. How is he?"

"Pensive."

"Hmm."

"So, you found your descendant all right, I assume?"

"Yes. Judas was the one behind the rebellion and his kidnapping."

He laughed. "Judas Iscariot?"

She nodded.

"Oh, that's hilarious."

"Speaking of things being hilarious, Gabriel told me about your run-in with the Nephilim."

"I was sleeping. He caught me off guard."

"Uh-huh."

"What's going on?" Will said, shuffling to the kitchen.

"Will, good of you to join us," Lucifer said.

"I'm just getting a snack." He pulled a box of cereal from the pantry and took a mixing bowl from the cabinet.

"Sit for a moment. Your girlfriend's Queen would like a word. If you'll both excuse me, I'm off to bed." He headed down the hall, leaving the two alone. Will sat, pouring the contents of the box into the bowl.

"What's up?"

She crossed her legs and cleared her throat. "I wanted to apologize for my behavior. I shouldn't have frightened you and locking Michelle in a cage was perhaps a little rash."

"You don't have to apologize. I know you're just doing it because you want to get back with my dad. It's okay. I'm not mad."

"You're not?"

He folded his hands and looked her in the eyes. "My dad never makes himself a priority. He gave up everything to make sure I grew up safe, including you. He worked a job that bored him in a place far away from everyone he cared about. He was lonely and miserable, but he didn't care because *I* was okay. He has more than earned the right to be with someone that makes him happy. I don't know if you're the best person for him, but I see how you look at him. Even when you were pissed off, it was clear how much you love him. I would be a crap son if I stood in the way of his happiness."

Her eyes softened. It was like she was looking at him for the first time. "You're a good son, Will. Your father obviously raised you well."

"Yes, he did. Oh, milk! Duh." He got up and went to the fridge just as Gabriel walked in.

"Dia," she said.

"I need to speak with you."

"Go ahead," Will said, pouring the milk and putting it back. "I'm gonna take this to my room. I'll probably pass back out as soon as I finish it."

"Night," Gabriel called after him as he left.

"Goodnight!" he called back as he closed the bedroom door behind him.

"Well?" Allydia asked.

"You're crazy."

"And?"

"And, it's a big ask."

"Can she do it?"

"I don't know. It's never been done."

"Messenger,"

"I understand. But, Jesus, Dia, are you sure?"

"I've fulfilled my commitment to your Father, yes?"

"Yes."

"Then, what do you care?"

"I care," Gabriel defended. "I consider us friends. Plus, my brother would never forgive me if--"

"Everything I do is for your brother. You can see into my past. You know my heart. Have I ever cared about anyone more than him?"

She softened her expression. "No."

"So, you will call your witch. Ask her to free me of this burden. Undo what has been done."

"All right. If that's what you want."

"You know that it is."

"Fine." She took her phone from her pocket and dialed Wendy's number.

"Can you do it?" Gabriel asked.

Wendy went to the desk and opened the drawer, waving her hand over the cat's eye necklace, removing its warding so she could access it. "Yeah, I can do it. I'll be right over." She ended the call and shoved the phone in her pocket before picking up a letter opener and jamming it into the tip of her finger, squeezing a few drops of blood onto the amulet. She took a deep breath and blew it out her mouth, not looking forward to the pain that would come with what she was about to do. The truth was, she'd put it off for too long already. Gabriel's friend needing help was the push she needed to get it over with. She braced herself against the wall. "Here goes nothin'." She took another breath and squeezed the necklace tight in her fist. "Solvo."

The cat's eye cracked open, spilling brilliant blue light from its center, filling the room with shimmering radiance. She tried to cover her eyes, but her arms were yanked down by the force of the magic. It spun around her, lifting her from the floor and turning her around as it blew through, forcing its way in. She cried out as her temperature rose, her skin flushing and her eyes glowing like bioluminescent algae. Her heartbeat was like a drum roll in her ears as she was pulled away from the wall and bent backward as much as her spine would allow as the last of the sparkling incandescence worked its way in through her open mouth as she screamed.

She dropped to the floor, the room going dark and the blue of her eyes returning to their normal shade. As her temperature went down and her heart rate settled, she caught her breath, never being so happy for something to be over in her life.

Chapter 27

Wendy lit the black candle with a red interior and placed it on the floor above Allydia's head as she lay in Gabriel's living room.

"Last chance to change your mind," Gabriel said from the ottoman.

"You sure?" Wendy asked.

Allydia nodded, folding her hands over her diaphragm and closing her eyes. "Proceed."

"All right then." She rubbed her hands together and held them over the vampire's chest, taking deep breaths as she prepared.

Yo, B, you should get over here, Gabriel thought to her brother.

Everything okay? he replied.

Dia's having Wendy do a spell on her. It's risky. She could die.

What? Stop her!

Can't. She begged to have it done.

I'm coming.

"Revorsio esse verus hominem," Wendy said. "Revorsio esse verus hominem." She repeated the phrase for several minutes as Allydia's body started to tremble.

"Is she okay?" Gabriel asked.

Wendy ignored her, continuing to chant. Allydia shook, her eyes rolling to the back of her head.

"Wendy, is she okay?!"

Wyatt burst in the door, racing to kneel next to the vampire opposite Wendy. "What are you doing to her?!" She kept chanting, her eyes twinkling like stars in shades of electric blue. Wyatt held Allydia's hand and touched her forehead. "She's burning up!" From underneath her skirt, a slow-moving puddle of blood emerged. "What the hell is happening?!"

"It's how she died," Gabriel told him, dropping to her knees next to him. "Uterine atony after childbirth." She placed a hand over her abdomen to heal it, but Wendy smacked it away. "Did she just--"

"REVORSIO ESSE VERUS HOMINEM!" Wendy fell back as the candle blew itself out and Allydia stopped moving. The witch caught her breath as she moved out of the way. "It's done."

Gabriel rushed around to take Wendy's spot across from her brother, put one hand over Allydia's abdomen, and the other on her head. Her skin glowed as her veins became visible. The angel looked pained as her hands began to shake. "This is taking too long." Her eyes met Wyatt's and he could see the worry in them as his heart beat out of his chest.

He squeezed Allydia's hand and brought it to his lips as a tear slid down his cheek. "Come back. Please, come back." Finally, a shallow breath escaped Allydia's throat, then another and another, each one deeper than the last. Gabriel backed away, lowering her head in relief as her friend's skin began to brighten, color returning to her face with more vibrancy than before. Wyatt breathed a sigh of relief and kissed her hand again.

"It worked?" Gabriel asked.

"Yep," Wendy said, standing up. "I need some water." She went to the kitchen and got a bottle from the fridge.

"What did she do?" Wyatt asked.

"She removed Lilith's spell. Put her back the way she was."

"You're kidding. You mean she's..."

"Human. A hundred percent regular-ass person. Hella dangerous. For a while there, I didn't think I'd be able to fix her." She got up and stomped to the kitchen. "You and I need to have a discussion about boundaries."

"You can't interrupt me mid-spell," Wendy defended.

"I wasn't interrupting, I was just trying to--"

"She had to be all the way back exactly as she was right before the original spell was done or it wouldn't have worked. You have to trust me on these things."

She sat on a stool and crossed her legs. "I'm working on it."

"Mm," Allydia moaned as she opened her eyes. "Wyatt," She reached up and touched his chin. "You're here."

He smiled through his tears, awash in emotion. "Yeah, I'm here. Why did you do this? You could have died."

"A risk worth taking."

"Why?"

"Forever without you would have been a pain worse than death. Besides, you need me."

"You didn't have to do this."

"Yes, I did."

He wiped his face and tucked her hair behind her ear. "I love you."

"And, I love you," She ran her fingertips over his lips. "More than anyone is ever going to."

He bent down and kissed her, cradling her face in his hands.

"Aw, that's sweet," Wendy commented.

Gabriel sighed. "Yeah, they're pretty cute when they're not dying or making me nauseous with their sex memories."

She laughed.

"Hey, were your eyes glowing earlier?"

"Probably."

"Freaky."

"Yeah."

"Is that common for you?"

"New development."

"Pretty impressive stuff you did tonight."

"I learned another trick while you were gone," Wendy teased.

"Really? Did you get a new spellbook?"

"No, I watched porn."

Gabriel laughed. "Well, we shouldn't let that education go to waste." They scampered off to Gabriel's bedroom, leaving Wyatt and Allydia alone to bask in the warmth of their reunion.

Chapter 28

Poe shot up in bed, her fluffy familiar sleeping soundly on the pillow next to her. Even from her Bourbon Street hotel room thirteen hundred miles away, she could feel Grace's magic being set free. There was no way the others didn't feel it, too.

She hopped out of bed and threw on a pair of jeans. She tossed the rest of her belongings in her backpack, not bothering to change her shirt from the one she'd been sleeping in, and looked up flights on her phone. She booked the soonest one and slipped her boots on, tying them as fast as she could. *What am I doing?* she thought. Grace's magic being released meant one of three things: Wendy needed it for a powerful spell and took it into herself, which was best-case scenario, Wendy activated it to protect herself from someone or something she couldn't handle on her own, *or* Julia somehow got her hands on it, killed Wendy, and used her blood to take the magic for herself. If Wendy was in trouble, there wasn't much she could do to help. She wasn't nearly as strong as a born-Tituban witch and she'd barely made it out of town alive last time she stood against Julia and her minions. Still, she had an obligation to try. Wendy only had Grace's magic because she brought it to her. It had been her mentor's dying wish, to see her family's magic passed to someone with Tituban blood. After she'd crossed over and her power was securely in the amulet, it acted as a compass, leading Poe directly to Wendy. She could have hidden it, sealed it away, and dropped it in the ocean. It's what she thought she *should* do. But, Grace was like a mother to her, and not honoring her wishes wasn't an option. Still, her stomach twisted with guilt as she smoothed the covers, leaving the room looking as nice as when she'd arrived.

"Come on, Raven," she said, patting the bed and holding open the pack. The bunny woke up and hopped over, climbing into the bag. "We're going home."

Julia looked up at the Tribeca apartment building, a shiver running down her spine as the remnants of magic emanating from four stories above lingered, dancing on the air like fireflies in the dark of the early morning. She couldn't tell who had activated Grace's magic, but whether it be Poe, an elder witch, or a stranger, there was one thing she was sure of: they wouldn't have it for long.

In the near distance, she heard the incessant cawing of a crow. She held out her arm as the bird swooped down and perched itself there, its weight a familiar comfort. "We've found it, Griffin," she told the animal. "Soon, Grace's magic will belong to us, as it was always meant to."

The End

The Complete Seventh Day Series

Seraphim
Nephilim
Elohim
Cain
Alukah
Coven
Sinclair

Printed in Great Britain
by Amazon